MILA'S SHIFT

MILA'S SHIFT

DANIELLE FORREST

The Eternal Scribe Publishing
Indianapolis, IN

The Eternal Scribe Publishing
www.theeternalscribe.com
theternalscribe@gmail.com

Cover Design: Amygdala Designs
Interior Design: Vellum
Printing: IngramSpark

First Edition
Paperback ISBN: 978-1-950795-00-0
Hardcover ISBN: 978-1-950795-01-7
Library of Congress Control Number: 2019941291

*M*ila took deep breaths to calm her pounding heart, anxiety eating her alive. She'd picked a table that backed up against a wall so no one could sneak up on her. The table sat on the café's patio on the far edge nearest the alley, perfect placement for a quick getaway.

Still, she felt exposed. Every set of eyes that lifted higher than their teacup or plate seemed to bore into her, questioning her, doubting her. Every Bluetooth headset made her wonder who listened on the other end of the line. And if that someone would shoot on sight.

Conversation washed over her, but she froze at the word "shifter" drifting on the wind.

A haughty feminine voice sneered and Mila caught the woman lifting a cup to her lips, so full of her own superiority. "They should all be shot."

Mila flinched, her hackles rising even more at the open hostility.

"Now, now, dear. There are no shifters near." He tried soothing her, but it was a futile task.

Mila held in her smirk.

"None near? Are you kidding?" She almost stood in her outrage, but her companion touched her hand, patting it until she settled. "A shifter could be sitting at this very cafe and we wouldn't have a clue!"

"Come now, Beatrix, the government screening is too good for that. Why, the news shows agents rounding more up every day. I saw with my own eyes one of them getting tossed into a van."

Beatrix grumbled into her cup, but her voice still carried to Mila. "The government couldn't round up their own asses."

Mila almost lost it, not sure if amusement or nerves played a bigger part in that moment. As the couple calmed, she blotted out their words. But nothing could erase the presence of two grotesque bigots sitting not three feet from her. It set her on edge, ready to run, ready to fight. She gritted her teeth, resisting the urge to beat the woman upside the head until she *really* had a reason to fear.

So when her friend, May, approached the cafe even more nervous than Mila, she raised an eyebrow.

Mila had spent her adult life on the wrong side of the law. She had good cause to be cautious. What did her law-abiding, goodie-two-shoes best friend have to fear?

Mila put on an awkward smile and called out, "Hey, May!"

Just like old times.

May's head jerked up after having scanned the tables and the street, not only looking for her, but also for a tail. Mila recognized it from experience. After all, she'd perfected the technique over the last ten years they'd been apart.

She wanted to apologize for leaving, for not explaining at

least. Instead, when her life had fallen to pieces, when she had to leave, she left a vague note to her twin in all but blood and walked out. She'd never expected to hear from her again.

Yes, Mila *wanted* to apologize, but how did one say, "I'm sorry for leaving, but I suddenly turned into a tiger, and I didn't know how to deal with that?" She almost laughed at the idea, what with the bigot at the next table.

Minutes passed with Mila lost in thought, something she knew far better than social situations anymore. May still stood behind the chair across from her, staring at Mila as if seeing a ghost.

She is, stupid.

Shaking her head at her own idiocy, Mila patted the glass surface next to her cup. "Come on, May. Sit." Though, honestly, her friend needed a bit more than a coffee and conversation right about now. Tequila shots might be in order.

May stood there, the rift between them heavy in the air. "Where have you been?"

Random abandoned buildings?

"Around," she said instead.

May scowled, but didn't push. Mila sat and stared, but the tension never left her friend's form, that awareness she knew so well feeling so alien on the other woman.

Why was May here?

And why was she so terrified?

Mila laughed. "Okay, maybe I shouldn't have had that second sandwich." Laughing again lightened her heart.

"Or maybe the half a chocolate cake you had for dessert," May said with a sly smile. It had taken a while, but May had relaxed little by little as they ate and talked.

It had been years since the best friends had been together. Mila had always maintained ways for the people she cared about to keep in touch with her, but never directly. She hadn't heard from anyone from her childhood in so long, it felt uplifting being a normal person for an hour.

Okay, maybe two.

"Yeah, but you can't count cake. Chocolate is a necessity, like air." A necessity she'd lacked for a long time.

May shook her head. "I don't understand how you can eat so much and not gain weight. You were like that in high school, but you haven't changed a bit, have you?"

"No, still got the metabolism from hell." Of course, May didn't know the reason for Mila's freakish metabolism. She didn't know that Mila needed excess energy to shift shape. Or that it gave her the ability to change fat into muscle. That was something she couldn't tell her friend. She trusted May, but May was an honest person, and she couldn't put that burden on her.

It was why she'd left that cryptic note, why she couldn't say goodbye in person. She loved May more than anyone else in the world, and she couldn't do that to her. Knowing May, she would have come with her, and at least one of them had to live their dream. Some days, nothing kept her going but that dream, the dream May lived for her.

May shook her head again. "I would *kill* to be able to eat that much. If I ate even a fraction of that, I'd be five hundred pounds!"

Mila stretched. "Ah, the blessings of being me."

They paid the checks, and Mila offered to walk May to her car. May had never mentioned why she'd reached out to her, and though the camaraderie had soothed them both, they remained on edge. Leaving the cafe, they turned down a small side road, tall buildings rising up on both sides like a canyon. May's car sat at the far end, she guessed. Only vehicle in sight.

Mila couldn't take the tension anymore. She had enough stress. She didn't need May's as well. "So, why did you *really* call me, May?"

May jumped and twisted sheepishly toward Mila. "What do you mean?"

"You haven't contacted me in ten years. Suddenly you reach out and you're skittish as a mouse? Something's wrong."

May wrung her hands, fidgeting from foot to foot, but she didn't speak. Mila gave her space, waiting her out. The words would come with patience.

Crashes of metal on metal, cheers, and lewd comments erupted from behind her. She turned as May's eyes grew wide. The raucous youths careened closer, pointing to the two women. Then cat calls echoed off the walls.

"Back slowly to the car, May." Mila's every nerve ramped up to a razor's edge. After ten years on the streets, she could sense trouble like a sixth sense. And these guys were bad news, big time. She started backing up, not watching where she was going, simply putting distance between her and the hooligans.

"Hey, don't leave!" one of them called.

"Yeah, we just wanna play!"

Cheers and crude gestures followed. Mila knew they were in trouble.

"Run," she whispered and turned to dash for the car. She shoved May before her and fled to the pounding beat of men in pursuit.

Her heart pounded anew, this time from exertion and fear rather than anxiety. As she ran, she focused on what she would need to survive this if it got messy. Strength. She'd need strength. She shifted every tissue she could to skeletal muscle. Years on the run, years spent hiding in old warehouses for fear of being seen, left her an expert at shifting.

As her arms pumped at her sides, she noted the increase in size and definition. It wouldn't be enough. She didn't have enough mass to get massive. But she had skill on her side. Another advantage of spending all her waking hours in a hole. She'd spent her free time practicing the martial arts she'd learned as a child and teenager.

Someone grabbed her arm and yanked it, pain shooting up her shoulder. A yelp flew from her mouth and she turned with the motion, using the guy's own grab against him and twisting him into an arm lock. She jerked her head to and fro, looking for other attackers, as the guy in her hands yelled and flailed. *Crack.* She slammed him hard on the back of the head and he crashed into the pavement.

Mila spun, searching for May, and screamed. "No!" She ran as the knife pulled from May's body, the red blood pouring out. She ran as her best friend's body fell in slow motion to the ground. Her limbs dragged at her like swimming through cement.

Mila skidded on her knees to her friend, grabbing her and pressing on the wound that pumped that life-giving liquid.

Pump, pump, pump. "You'll be okay, May. You're gonna be okay."

Wetness coated her cheeks before she realized she'd been crying. She tried to wipe the tears away, but her sticky hands smeared blood across her face.

The pace of that pumping slowed, slowed, and stopped. An eternity stretched as she waited for it to pump again, for more blood to gush out, but nothing. "No. No. She can't be." She covered her face with her bloody palms, shaking her head and denying the truth before her. "No, no, no."

After a time, the tears ceased. Numbness settled in as she rocked her friend, her other half. Soon, the numbness evaporated too, and the fog in her head dissipated, her predicament becoming clear. She couldn't call the cops. As a shifter, they would either arrest her or shoot on sight, depending on the officer. There was no ambiguity in the law on shifters. The government didn't know what to do with them, so they'd passed a law making it illegal to be a shifter.

Not like she had a choice in the matter.

Mila would never go to those camps. Even living her entire life in abandoned buildings held more appeal.

She couldn't call the cops. She couldn't report May's murder. Besides, Mila believed May wouldn't have wanted Mila to be taken. Not for her. She took a deep breath and hated herself a little. She grabbed May's keys and popped the trunk.

What else could she do?

Hours passed as she found what she needed, found the right spot, and laid her friend to rest. She thought of leaving her friend's body somewhere conspicuous, but it felt wrong to abandon her that way. She cried the entire time she dug the hole. Patting down the last of the dirt, she tilted her head to the dark sky. The same words kept passing through her mind like a marquee.

I'm sorry.

Mila sat in the driver's seat, staring at the bag next to her. When she'd been deciding what to bury May with, she'd gone through it.

May had a verified ID.

Her conscience warred with her logic. Her conscience told her it was wrong. Her logic told her May wouldn't need it anymore. What was the harm? Her conscience just kept telling her it was wrong, but her brain, her logic, kept coming up with new reasons to do it. She wouldn't have to run and hide. She could have a normal life. May was a pilot just like she'd trained to be. Nobody would ever have to know. She could have a life.

Pulling the ID from the bag, she stared at it. She stared until it almost mesmerized her, until her vision blurred, refocused and blurred once more. She knew she would do it. The ship left in less than twenty-four hours.

No one would ever have to know.

And one of them had to live their dream…

CHAPTER TWO

er body felt strange, foreign, like it had a mind of its own. Her brain swam inside the cage of her uncooperative flesh. Muffled shouts and jeers drifted into her fuzzy brain. Spikes of adrenaline shot through a system that simply wanted to slump against one of these nice, comfy cars and fall asleep.

Or throw up. Her stomach lurched, threatening to unleash the countless shots of vodka she'd had that night. She held her middle, willing it to settle. *I'm never drinking again.*

Her mind flitted around like a bug in a jar. She leaned her weight against the cold, slick metal, tempted to lean her face against it, hoping the icy surface would soothe her.

"Sweetness," a slurred male voice said, making it through the murk.

She jerked up and almost fell over, catching herself against the nearest object. Her arm slammed against cold metal, pain radiating from the point of contact. A wall of men closed in, activating some far-off warning system in her psyche, like hearing an ambulance coming but not knowing where.

When had they gotten so close?

One grabbed her from behind, wrapping an arm around her waist.

Everything inside her rebelled, fighting and screaming all at once.

<hr>

Mila jerked awake, breathing hard. For a spell, she stayed in that moment so many years ago, leaving May behind, leaving her career behind. A single tear ran down her face.

Why am I crying?

Hadn't she cried out all these emotions years ago? Back then, the world felt impossible, too much to cope with alone.

Then she remembered.

May was dead.

She sucked in a shuddering breath and the tears came in earnest this time. They poured a deluge until her face burned with the emotion, her nose stuffed worse than any cold. The rivers of salty sorrow dried to an arid riverbed. A hollowed out shell, she sat there on the mattress, the once wet tracks leaving tight reminders on her skin.

Getting out of bed, Mila dressed on autopilot, falling back into the old routines with ease, but stopped dead when she reached the door to the bathroom. A part of her refused to force her feet forward.

She couldn't do it. She couldn't look in the mirror and see May's face. It would break her. Minutes ticked by where she tried to quiet the turmoil inside. After a time, she crossed the threshold with her head downcast, her—no, May's—hair blocking the view. She did what she had to, grabbed what she needed, and raced out as if her life depended on it.

Mila dropped on the bed with a gasp, needing a few more moments to center herself. "I am May. I am May Trace," she chanted again and again, tears recurring and choking her. Not capable of keeping her own company right now, she turned on the TV, hoping it could silence the pain eating her alive.

"I wouldn't say it's a controversy," the man on screen said, steepling his fingers in front of him. "It's a question of basic human rights."

"Yet, they're not human, are they?"

Mila flinched, but couldn't look away.

"Aren't they? Do we know they're not?"

"Yet it's a proven fact that they're a danger. They can change into anyone, anything. One could change into the President and just walk right into the White House, or a military base, or our schools." The screen shifted to a female leaning forward in outrage.

"First, the government takes steps to prevent that. No one can get into a secured facility without a verified ID, and many places without on site DNA confirmation. Our country *is* secure."

The woman grumbled. "But that doesn't change them from stealing other identities. No one is safe until these criminals are brought to justice."

"Criminals? Really?" The man supporting shifters balked. "You're trying to tell me that Emmaline Grayson was a criminal?" The video changed to a scene of a teenager being dragged away. She fought like anyone would, but the men easily overpowered her, hurting her. She slumped in their arms and even from the grainy footage, Mila could see blood.

"What did she, an honor roll high school student, do to deserve such treatment? What justifies stealing a child from her home, beating her, and leaving her hospitalized?"

"Come now," the woman scoffed, "that is one instance of police brutality."

The shifter supporter leaned forward. "Thirty-four percent of shifters in the camps are underage. They're children too unaware of what they are to even know to hide it."

Mila flinched, the statement hitting too close to home. She shut it off. She didn't want to hear how much the world hated her kind, how bad others had it, or more importantly, what her fate would be if she got caught.

Mila rubbed her hands on May's pants as she fidgeted in line, May's bag digging into her shoulder. *This will work. They won't question a verified ID.* She tried not to stare in awe at the giant spacecraft looming in the background. It was a veritable antique, from back when ships could still enter atmosphere. It had a MAG GRAV system, for crying out loud.

A half hour later, a woman in uniform glanced at May's ID, then up at Mila's face, which now matched May's. Satisfied, she barked a bunk and station assignment at her before telling her to report to med bay. Mila dashed off, following the guy before her. *May would want this.*

He hadn't been able to confirm the kill. Without the confirmation, he didn't get paid. He'd orchestrated that attack to make it look like a mugging gone wrong, but his lackeys fled before they knew for certain May Trace was no more.

So now he sat, scope steady and ready, monitoring each person who boarded the ship, searching for the one who didn't belong. The one who should be dead. Emergency services never found a body, and neither she nor any Jane Does showed up at the ER.

His left side had long since gone numb when his scope zeroed in on her, twitching in line.

His job wasn't finished.

Kyle Avery walked beside the captain as they ambled through the ship, discussing security protocols and the mission—in as vague terms as possible. They both knew the stakes. If this mission didn't succeed…

They passed crew members and guests, the uniforms blending into a seamless mob as intended. But as he walked by one woman, he looked behind himself and stopped, something sending all his instincts on alert. She raced away, harried like everyone else. No one was familiar with this model of ship anymore so most of the crew would struggle for a few days getting accustomed to the layout.

But something just felt *off* about her. He couldn't put his finger on it, though. Same uniform, nondescript hair, everything seemed regulation, no different from anyone else on board, but something told him she didn't belong.

"Avery?"

He spun on his heels. "Yes, Captain?"

"Is something wrong?"

He turned around, but she'd disappeared around a corner. "No, Captain." He continued walking, keeping pace with

Captain Faulk. He didn't know what to think. She had felt off, wrong, but he didn't have that gut-wrenching feeling he got when a mission went FUBAR. He didn't believe she was a threat—just a mystery.

Mila's gut felt like she'd swallowed acid, maybe hydrochloric acid. Or that stuff they use to dissolve mortar.

Chaos.

Medical personnel and security staff lined the walls of the med bay, standing at little temporary tables with QuiKits. Every few seconds, someone would bark out, "Next," and the line would move forward.

Mila was losing her shit. The same thing kept running through her brain. *What are they testing for?* Was it to confirm identity? But no, QuiKits couldn't do genomic identity testing. And they couldn't do identity testing onboard. The databases required to store the data would be enormous, and running that much information through secured connections took time, even today. Checking against billions and billions of bases took a long, long time, no matter how powerful your computer system.

But QuiKits *could* test for specific genotypes. It could test for shifters. If it tested that, she was dead. She wanted to open her mouth. She wanted to ask someone what was going on, what they were testing for, but knew it would spell her doom if she did.

She was a freak. Even excluding her shifter status, no one else had come onboard clueless. She didn't know their mission, didn't know their protocols, didn't know shit.

Mila hadn't served in the NSS for ten years. In fact, she'd *never* served in the NSS since she'd never finished her training.

Someone barked, "Next," and Mila realized no one stood in front of her.

She walked up to the only open station and took a deep breath, too worried to look the guy in the eye.

"Hand," he said as he busied himself opening the kit.

Mila stuck her arm out and sneaked a peek at the packaging. "QuiKit: STD Panel," it read, and she let out a breath.

Big black block letters marked every corridor, so Mila only made one wrong turn before finding her bunk. Two beds were bolted to the wall of the tiny room, one on top of the other, and two wardrobes abutted the opposite wall. Nothing else. Her arms and shoulders skimmed the wardrobes and metal bed frame as she walked down the middle. She almost hunched sideways to get around the ladder to the top bunk.

"Hi," she said to her roommate. "Name's May Trace." She'd been practicing using the name ad nauseam over the last twenty-four hours. She repeated it in her head even now. "I'm a pilot."

Her roommate glanced up before continuing to unpack. "Santos. Comms," she said.

Mila ignored the snub and unloaded her bag into her wardrobe, latching everything down.

MAG GRAV systems prevented bone loss, but paled in comparison to modern systems. They didn't produce gravity. Instead, they used magnetics to simulate the force gravity puts on your body. Any non-magnetic items would fly everywhere once they left Earth.

Mila nodded and headed off to her duty station. She had first shift on the bridge. Though everything else terrified her, she looked forward to flying. She hadn't flown in so long, she wasn't sure she would remember how.

What if she failed? Sub-space travel took skill, a skill she hadn't practiced in far too long.

But even with a sea of doubt coursing through her head, she walked to the bridge with a grin on her face.

For a military ship, slipping aboard proved no challenge at all. Once onboard, he grabbed the first person he found alone, dragged him into a quiet corridor, and snapped his neck. He took in the details, then started his shift.

As a whole, the Orleans might have been old and under-whelming, but stepping onto the bridge would always fill Mila with awe. It brought a huge smile to her face as she stepped into the room. There was a time she'd lived for this moment. The expansive view, the consoles, the controls, even the captain sitting in his chair looking almighty and, she was ashamed to say, hot.

After high school, she and May had trained as pilots. It had been one of the best times of her life, maybe *the* best. Flying had been her dream and her gift. They'd dreamed of shipping out together, flying side by side, even if it was a ridiculous fantasy.

But Mila had shifted before she ever flew outside simulators.

In training, she'd bested every record, but people didn't hire shifters. That drunken night ten years ago ended her life. She ran. She never stopped running.

Until now.

<hr>

Out of necessity, Captain Tristan Faulk was on edge. He watched as each person entered the bridge, waiting for word from his Lieutenant on their status. Some personnel he'd worked with before. Others were new to him

His attention zeroed in on a female officer who swaggered onto the bridge as if she owned the thing. She stopped, her face stretching into a smile he found contagious, then sashayed to the pilot's seat.

His gut sent him mixed signals about the girl. On the one hand, he couldn't get his eyes to drift away from how her ass swayed in those tight uniform pants. On the other, his instincts screamed that she wasn't military. Something about her was wrong. Maybe she had attitude problems. Still, he would check out her file when he got back to his quarters. And he would keep an eye on her from here on out.

On her, not her butt.

<hr>

Mila sat, waiting for the order to take off. An effervescent sensation bubbled up inside her. She feared she would start giggling at any moment. Nothing would give her away faster than a pilot with a giggling fit.

She cracked her knuckles, rolled her neck, and stretched every muscle group she could think of. A guy next to her couldn't stop smiling at her. At least he wasn't laughing.

Mila waited as people around her went about their business. Some raced about, preparing for take off, but many twiddled their thumbs just like her.

While she leaned back in her seat, an officer—high ranked based on the amount of crap on his uniform—spoke to the captain, and took his position. The captain leaned forward and said, "Okay, everyone, final pre-flight checks."

Mila went though the motions. It had been years, but she told herself it was like riding a bike. She could do this in her sleep, even if doubt kept creeping in.

She put the panel in pre-flight mode, and ran her fingers over the controls, testing their responses. Flaps. Check. Propulsion. Check. Yoke response. Check. She continued through the checklist to the end, then turned and reported to the captain, "Pilot pre-flights complete, captain." Mila took the controls out of pre-flight mode.

Others echoed her sentiment, the echo growing with each voice. The sounds merged, building toward something. Mila almost held her breath, waiting and eager for the good part. After a few minutes, everyone had reported in.

"All right. Let's take this baby out. Communications, please confirm our flight status with the tower."

"Yes, captain," a guy several stations down from her said. He spoke into the radio, then turned to the captain. "We're cleared for take off, captain."

"Take off, pilot."

"Yes, captain," Mila said, a great big smile on her face.

Finally.

The USS Orleans was temperamental at the best of times. Tristan watched, almost in awe, as the pilot maneuvered the behemoth into space. She flew as if the Orleans were a fighter jet, not the largest ship that could leave Earth's surface, a ship so old the engines practically rattled.

Impressive.

And for a moment, he forgot his suspicion of her.

Which left room for other concerns to surface. Like the mission. He liked being a captain, running his crew. He enjoyed the responsibility, the authority. But he'd avoided this type of assignment his entire career, not that command had ever offered him one.

His thoughts strayed to the diplomats hidden among the crew. They'd been breathing down his neck since they'd arrived on board, but he'd kicked them out of the bridge, telling them he couldn't have the distractions.

Liar.

He didn't *want* the distractions.

His gaze roved back to the pilot. Her graceful arms shifted from one control to the next. Once they cleared Earth, they would enter sub-space. Faster-than-light travel didn't exist. Messages could travel faster than light, but any matter that attempted it didn't reach the other end in the same condition as it departed.

The discovery of sub-space allowed for interstellar travel. Sub-space didn't act like normal space did. Like how tachyonic particles didn't follow the same rules as normal particles, sub-space had its own unique set of rules. One of those rules made it possible to travel many light years in a matter of months.

"Entering sub-space momentarily," she said, her hands still flying over the controls.

He loved this part. Around him, the universe bent and contorted like a funhouse mirror. Then it righted itself as they arrived in sub-space, but this place brought to mind the other side of Alice's mirror. Nothing seemed quite right. Distances seemed distorted, visual range shifted. Many pilots had difficulty flying in sub-space. Many others couldn't and never received credentials for off-planet flight.

But this pilot traversed the surreal landscape of sub-space as if it were no big thing. Planets, moons, and asteroids flew toward them at speed. Sub-space seemed a compression of normal space, with distances between objects reduced. It meant navigation could be tricky if planets were close. Even hundreds of millions of miles apart in normal space could end up so close that a large ship like the Orleans maneuvered between them with difficulty.

But gravity wasn't a problem in sub-space. It didn't exist in sub-space the same way it did in normal space, leaving planets and stars misshapen and bloated. A pilot could come as close as one wished to a planet without fearing being sucked into its gravitational field.

He winced as they passed close to a planet's rings, but relaxed when nothing happened. The pilot never even batted an eye at the near miss. Either she knew her skills well or she was utterly insane.

His new persona didn't work the first shift. Unfortunately, his target did. At the doorway to the bridge, he leaned against a wall out of sight, but close enough to keep tabs on her. He had patience.

He would finish the job.

<hr>

Once her shift ended, she followed her roommate, Santos, to the mess hall. After picking up a tray of something that vaguely resembled food, she approached Santos, the only person she knew on this boat. "Mind if I sit with you?"

Santos shrugged and continued eating.

So much for conversation.

Mila dug in. At least she could say that while it looked like gruel, it didn't taste bad. Behind her, people spouted hate, and Mila tried to ignore it, but failed.

"They're just a bunch of fucking monsters," one guy said.

"I hear they can't even enter our atmosphere. Why would we ally ourselves with weaklings like that?"

"I know, right?"

"Hello, my buds!" A guy sat down next to them, distracting her from the venom behind her.

He must work a later shift. She looked over at him between bites and realized it was the guy who'd been sitting next to her on the bridge. He had a big, goofy smile on his face. She couldn't for the life of her figure out how he had so much energy after working eight hours.

"Luke Hall, communications," he said, reaching out his hand for a handshake.

Mila, she almost said. "May Trace, pilot."

"Well, it's a pleasure to fly with you, May. That was some smooth sailing." His entire body communicated with him.

"Thanks. So, you're both in communications?"

"I'm the maths guy. She's the computer genius."

"Cool."

Mila didn't understand the TAT system. It required both a mathematician and a computer scientist to operate. If they made a mistake, it could alter the rules of the universe, breaking cause and effect.

Yeah, oops.

But on the plus side, they could send real-time messages with Earth… so long as they didn't fuck up the calculations.

Not that she had anyone to send messages to. She thought of her parents, but they probably thought she was dead.

Like May.

Mila shook her head, trying to tear the morbid thought from her psyche. She had to snap out of it. She couldn't keep doing this to herself.

"So," Luke said, rubbing his hands together, "who's up for a game of poker?"

Santos jumped right in. Mila stared, surprised at her roommate's zeal, but agreed as well.

A few hours, and a shameful sum of money lighter, Mila excused herself to head back to her bunk. Her skin crawled from the amount of social interaction she'd incurred. Sure, she kept to herself on the bridge, but she'd socialized more in the canteen than she had in years.

She passed a couple women talking between themselves as she reached her bunk assignment.

"The Incirrina just scare the crap out of me. I mean, what do they want? Nobody wants nothing fcr something, ya' know?"

"That's for the government to handle. Just focus on your job."

"But what if they want to invade?"

"Remember? They can't enter our atmosphere. How could they possibly invade?"

Mila entered her bunk, sighing and relaxing into the door when it closed behind her, closing off the rest of the ship.

Hopefully, her roommate wouldn't return until she'd taken everyone's money.

He was unfortunate enough to have picked someone on the worst shift for trying to catch his target alone. As soon as Trace's shift ended, his started. By the time he got off shift, she was asleep in her bunk, which had privacy locks. He'd checked, and the locks were engaged. He might have to pick another identity if he couldn't find an opportunity soon.

"So, what do you think of her? I like her," Luke said with gusto. Her money had dwindled to almost nothing in front of her. She'd never felt less deserving of her nickname, Lucky, in her life. She looked across the table to the orrery Santos's pile. It looked like a dragon's treasure. And she had the attitude to match. Pity, because if Luke were into girls, she would totally go for that dark skin and exotic eyes.

"I don't know. There's something not quite right about her."

"Ah," Luke said, waving her hand, "she's just a free spirit.

Your uptight military ass just can't handle that much awesomeness."

Santos glared at her.

———

Tristan settled into his office and pulled up the personnel files on all the pilots on board. Only one was female. May Trace. As he skimmed through the file, he got more suspicious. No demerits, no nothing. That he could tell, nothing made May Trace stand out. She'd never been in trouble, which didn't mesh with the woman he'd glimpsed today.

But, more than that, her file listed her as a mediocre pilot. Good enough for approval for interstellar travel, but unexceptional. His gut told him something wasn't right, but he couldn't put his finger on it. Trace was far too good a pilot to match her files.

CHAPTER THREE

$\mathcal{L}$uke greeted Mila at her bunk like a two hundred pound puppy dog. He wrapped his arm around hers and dragged her to the bridge.

When they arrived, her gaze slid to the captain as he gave her an odd look. She looked away and relieved the pilot. All shift, that moment plagued her, taunting her with the potential inner workings of the captain's mind.

She couldn't afford any scrutiny. She ducked her head, kept quiet, and resumed piloting the POS, as she liked to call the USS Orleans. The thing belonged in a scrap yard, not flying in sub-space.

Mila tried not to show it, but anxiety was eating a hole through her gut. She couldn't escape. She knew it. They would catch her, find out what she was, then dump her out the airlock, or shoot her. The scenarios rotated on an endless loop, tormenting her with the unknown.

I talk too much, Luke thought as she chatted up the pilot next to her. *Or maybe May's just too damned terse.* But that didn't stop her from trying to engage her neighbor in conversation. Like a teenage girl, Luke couldn't sit more than two minutes without words bubbling up her throat and spewing into existence like a bad case of food poisoning. Her mom called it "cute." She often said, "That's my Lucky," with a soft smile on her face.

Luke didn't think it was cute, though. She thought it was a pain. She'd tried, honestly tried, but every time she kept quiet, all her insecurities rose up to choke her. Like voices from her past, they taunted her, tormented her, made her feel less human. If she kept inside her own head for too long, she would go mad.

She often wondered if there was something wrong with her. She'd spent more time than she could count staring at that DSM definition, reading the signs and symptoms. But a diagnosis would be the easy way out. The military would pay for it then. "Only when medically necessary," the policy read. Or, in other words, only when you were about to off yourself.

Luke didn't want to die, not even close. She loved her life, loved being in the NSS. Most of the time. Other careers would have been easier for someone like her. Other careers didn't have communal showers or zero privacy. She shuddered at the very thought. Never again. She never wanted to be called a freak again.

"Oh my God, look at that planet," she said, distracting herself. She nudged May, but the other woman just glared at her. Luke shrugged. She would get her to warm up, eventually.

After a few hours, Luke managed to drag Mila from her shell. She spent the rest of her shift half paying attention to flying and half paying attention to him. Mila could fly this ship through sub-space sleep deprived, with one eye closed, and with a lobotomy, so chatting wasn't a problem.

She liked Luke. He didn't take himself too seriously, and was a tad loose with the rules. If she didn't strangle him for talking too much, she could see them becoming good friends. He was a normal person in a sea of military uptightness.

A constant litany of terrible outcomes flowing through her mind put a damper on the day, though. That and the captain's intense gaze boring into the back of her skull.

"Finally!" Luke said as he stretched. "That felt like forever."

Mila rolled her eyes at him. "Please, it wasn't any different from yesterday."

She stood and headed to the door, but someone stepped in her way.

"Can I help you, sir?"

He looked down at her name embroidered on her uniform. "Trace? We don't take slacking lightly on this ship. You're the pilot. You hold the lives of everyone on board in your hands when you're at the helm. I expect you to give your utmost when on duty. Today was unacceptable. Do you understand?"

"Yes, sir," Mila grumbled.

"Don't let it happen again," he said and stepped aside.

After they'd turned a couple corners, she asked, "Who the hell does he think he is?"

"Lieutenant Braddock. He's directly under the captain. It would probably be best to stay out of his way."

Mila smirked at Luke. "Oh, I'm fantastic at staying out of the way."

He smiled back. "I get the feeling you're gonna be *very* fun to be around."

"Always."

———

"What was that?" Captain Faulk said as his second in command came up to his shoulder.

"Just reprimanding a wayward crew member, sir."

"For what?" he replied, trying to think of what mistake she'd made during the shift. Or maybe it was something he hadn't seen, something she'd done behind his back.

"Not giving her position the necessary respect and attention, sir. Piloting in sub-space is not an idle task, as you well know, and I won't have pilots slacking off on shift."

"Lieutenant?"

"Yes?"

"Whose ship is this?"

"Yours, sir."

"I suggest you remember that." He stood up, and nodded to his second in command, wishing he'd had a better option. "You have the bridge."

"Aye, sir."

———

She kept shoveling dirt, but no matter how much she dug, it

never seemed to be enough. Beside her, May kept saying, "I thought we were sisters, twins. I thought you loved me."

"I do," Mila said, wanting to rub the tears off her face but compelled to keep digging.

She had to do it.

For May.

She had to.

"Why did you do this to me, Mila?" her friend said.

Mila gasped awake, banging her head on the ceiling. "A dream," she breathed, "It was only a dream."

She rubbed her eyes, wiping the tears away, but it didn't make the heat abate.

Or the pain.

"Come on. We'll be late. You don't need two demerits in as many days."

"I'm coming. I'm coming," he said, gasping as he raced after his friend. *When did I get so out of shape?*

His companion let out a sigh of relief as they slammed through the galley doors. "Looks like we didn't get caught. Head cook isn't here."

"See? No reason to worry."

"Buddy, they already demoted you to cook. Next step is out of the service."

"With my history? Might be a better option." He looked around. "I'm gonna go restock."

" 'Kay."

He turned and walked deeper into the galley area. The next room contained two doors for the walk-ins, a refrigerator and a freezer. He yanked hard on the lever to open the freezer. Like always, it fought him. "Come on, you stupid piece of shit." He lost his balance when the door flew open. "Stupid old-assed ship."

He entered, turning his head back and forth. Not having memorized the layout yet, he suffered under the sadist who'd arranged the galley storage for this trip. He turned around the end of an aisle and stopped, stumbling over something on the floor. *Odd.* They had to strap everything down to prevent zero gravity from making a mess. Nothing should have been paired.

The object was mostly shoved under a shelf and covered in a thin layer of ice, just like everything else. He scoffed. They had the freezer set too low. "Just my luck. I bet *I'm* gonna be the one freezing my ass off in here prying shit off the shelves."

He sighed and knelt, yanking at the obstacle, wondering who'd been too lazy to put things in their proper place. For once, it hadn't been him. He could enjoy someone else getting reamed out for a change.

When the cloth-wrapped object gave, he screamed as recognition hit. He slammed into the back wall in shock, scrambling for the handle. He couldn't take his eyes off the macabre visage. *Where the fuck's the door?!* "Fuck."

His hand slapped over cold metal, but no handle. "Fuck, fuck, fuck," but he couldn't get himself to look away, like a sick, twisted car wreck, it demanded he slow down and look.

How could he not look?

How could anyone not look?

Chills raced down his spine and it had nothing to do with the sub-zero temperatures. The plastic button connected with his palm and he smacked it hard, the door giving way under his weight. He ran out, not looking back, not that it mattered. He would never forget.

"What the hell's wrong with you?" his friend asked.

He tried to catch his breath, but he felt like he'd run a fucking marathon. "Buh, buh, buh," kept coming from his lips, not quite forming the word. He bent over, sucking in great, big gasps that didn't sting from cold. "Body," he said, "Dead body."

CHAPTER FOUR

"What have we got?" Captain Faulk said.

"Well, a dead body," the medical officer replied as he warmed his hands from the frigid air.

The captain glared at him. "You know what I meant."

"Well, someone dumped him in a freezer, so I have no way of knowing when he died, at least not by normal means like liver temp and decomposition."

Tristan pointed to one of his security officers. "Have we got an ID yet?"

"Yes, sir. He was last seen a couple hours ago."

"What?" the medical officer said, disbelief in his voice.

"What is it?" Tristan asked.

"Sir, I need to take the body back to medical, but I think it's too frozen to have been in there only a couple hours. It's hard on the outside. I don't know how much of his tissue is frozen, but I don't think that could have happened so fast. I fish back home, and it takes *hours* to freeze a fish whole."

"Do you have any idea what you're implying?" Tristan snarled.

"Yes, sir. We may have a shifter on board. And it has no qualms about killing."

"You," Tristan barked at another one of his security officers. "Find this shifter before it assumes a new identity." He turned to everyone else. "*No* one speaks of this. I can't have information about this body leaking until we catch this thing."

A chorus of "yes, sirs" echoed back at him.

———

He left his station to run an errand for a superior officer. With any luck, it would give him an opportunity to take out Trace.

As he walked down the corridor, an entourage of security officers pounded down the hall. He ducked around a corner as they passed, waiting. They ignored him as people often did. His eyes picked up everything. A cloud of tension hovered over them. Several men near the center of the grouping carried a bundle between them.

Trouble.

When they moved out of sight, he changed course. He had to check. He diverted to the mess hall, slipped in without a sound, and listened, waited.

Dissonant voices bounced off the old industrial walls, chairs scraped, and no one paid attention to the assassin in the corner. *There.* May Trace sat at a table near the middle of the room. He could kill her, but it wouldn't be a clean getaway. Not yet. He needed to get her alone.

He focused again on his current goal. Tucking his chin and

scrunching his shoulders, he made his way to the galley. Again, he listened, pushing the door ajar to hear better.

"You would not believe what I saw."

"I know what you saw. I saw them taking him out of here."

"It's no fair. They ordered me to keep quiet."

"Which clearly you're incapable of doing."

"Hey!"

"What? It's the truth."

"Yeah, but…"

"No but. I'm amazed they haven't canned you yet."

"Come on. It's not every day you find a dead body in a freezer."

I knew it. They found the body. Now compromised, he needed a new identity. Fast.

***

Mila followed Luke to the mess hall, only half listening to his idle banter. She hadn't been serious when she'd joked about her encounter with Braddock. She couldn't afford to be on Braddock's radar. That could get her killed.

Here, she didn't know how to keep a low profile, though. Usually, she just found an abandoned building and cut off all contact with others. As a strategy, hiding worked well on the run, but not so well stuck on a ship with a bunch of people who carried firearms.

She could stop talking on shift, like she had that first day. Keep her head down. Do nothing to draw attention. But was it too late?

"Whoa, what's this?" Luke said.

Mila glanced up and into the eyes of Captain Faulk. A chill ran down her spine as he seemed to stare right into her, seeing her darkest secrets. He and his battalion of security officers continued to barrel forward as she stopped in place, slack-jawed and terrified.

Oh, shit. They know.

CHAPTER FIVE

*L*uke grabbed Mila's arm and yanked her out of the way. "Jeez, May, they almost trampled you there."

"Sorry," she said when her voice finally worked and the captain and his men continued onward, intent on whatever mission wasn't her. She let out a heavy breath. "God, he scares the shit out of me."

"Haha. Well, I've been watching him. Communications isn't as intense as piloting. I think he's attracted to you."

Her jaw dropped again. "You've got to be fucking kidding me."

He shrugged. "Just calling 'em as I see 'em."

Mila shook her head. "Maybe you should stick to comms and idle banter. Matchmaking isn't your forte."

Someone knocked at Tristan's door.

"Come in."

"Sir?" A familiar face peeked in through the gap. He walked all the way in, his stance, his demeanor, screaming civilian. "I'm concerned about the mission."

"I won't allow it to fail. You have my word on that."

"But security on board. I have concerns. I heard one of your men was killed today."

Tristan frowned at the man intruding on his limited down-time. "I assure you everything is under control."

"If this mission doesn't succeed…"

Tristan stood, his chair grinding against the floor. "I know full well the ramifications if we were to fail. We *won't* fail. We can't."

"But…"

"Is that all?"

"What's your plan?"

"I have plans to capture this assassin."

"Assassin! Are you kidding me?! There's an assassin on board?"

"We believe so. The medical officer believes the man was dead long before he was last seen."

"A shifter." The diplomat fell to the closest seat in shock.

Tristan sighed. "Yes. And if we don't find it soon, it will take another identity. It will kill again."

The civilian uttered a curse word Tristan had never heard before, then stood. "I guess I'm in the way then."

"It would be easier to do my job without repeated interruptions, yes."

"I'll go back to my quarters."

"Good night."

"Good hunting, captain."

Mila didn't say much at dinner. Luke, his ever-talkative self, didn't even notice. Santos didn't care. After a respectable time period, she excused herself. Tonight, it was just too difficult to pretend everything was normal.

Too close. It had been too close. And she'd just stood there frozen in the hallway. If they'd actually been hunting her, they could have shot her, arrested her, anything and she would have done nothing to stop them.

What's wrong with me?

She wandered back to her room with a head full of toxic thoughts. Then someone grabbed her by the back of the neck and slammed her into an alcove, smashing her face into the metal wall. She flailed, kicked, punched, panic invalidating all her years of training. Her heart pounded away, making her stupid, jerky, useless. Her chest compressed with all she felt, most of it indescribable in the moment. But she never stopped moving.

Don't stop.

Don't stop.

Just fight.

A lucky knee found its target and he groaned, holding himself and bending over in perfect invitation for another hit. No longer on the defensive, her mind cleared. *Don't mind if I do.* She slammed her elbow into the back of his head, sending him to the floor, where he groaned again, but didn't move.

She took off, convinced he would follow at a moment's notice.

Safety.

Need safety.

People.

Anything.

She turned a corner and stumbled onto a common room. Flying through the doorway, she erupting into a space filled with other personnel. Nobody noticed as she desperately caught her breath, sucking in great gasps. Nobody noticed the blood on her face, or the darkening bruise she felt forming.

Relax.

Be cool.

Mila walked to the other side of the room, trying not to draw attention. She would be safe with an entire room of people separating her from her attacker. She sat down, shaking from adrenaline and fear. Her gaze stayed glued to the door.

After a few minutes that felt like hours, the door opened and her foe stood there, watching her, waiting. He smiled, raised his eyebrows, and ran his finger over his throat before walking away.

Oh, fuck.

CHAPTER SIX

Mila headed back to her bunk when someone she recognized as living near her left the common room. She slipped behind him and never allowed more than a few feet between them. Her heart pounding in her ears, fear kept her from wondering what he thought of her following him. She tried to move smoothly down the hall, but her limbs jerked on her joints.

What had May gotten her into? And it had to be May, right?

Once in her room, she went to bed but didn't sleep. She continued to shake, her mind running over all the fates that could befall her.

Who was he? What did he want? He couldn't have found out she was a shifter. She'd been careful, hadn't she? But May was a good girl. What could she have done to make someone want to kill her?

Hours later someone stumbled in, but she still hadn't fallen asleep. Mila didn't make a noise. She didn't look. Fear and her personal demons turned the intruder into her mysterious attacker. *Don't be stupid. It's just Santos. Nobody else can get in here.*

Could they?

———

Mila woke with a start. She felt like crap. Avoiding Santos, she grabbed her stuff and slipped out to the communal showers, heart in her throat. *Oh, God. What if he attacks me in the shower?* Her pulse ratcheted up another notch. Her mind shifted the images to him attacking her, water beating down on her, slipping on the wet tiles, cracking her head. The hallway took on sinister qualities, every person, every shadow signaling her premature demise.

But she opened the door to steam and laughter. *Get over it, Mila.* It still weirded her out showering next to guys, or anyone really. The military had long stopped caring about separating men and women. After all, it wasn't possible to separate people who might enjoy the eyeful.

Mila dropped the towel and walked to a stall. Her ridiculous shower was quick and her eyes didn't leave the shower head if she could help it.

She'd discovered something new…

She hated zero gravity showers. How was a person supposed to feel clean when the water just floated and beaded up rather than flowing over you? She finished, dried off, struggling over the magnetic bands that kept her paired to the floor. Wrapping the towel back around her, she dashed out, avoiding the wall of mirrors.

Even trying not to pay attention, she registered a few odd looks in the bathroom, in the hall. She slipped into her room, grateful for the privacy. Santos had already left. She sighed.

Alone.

Good.

She got dressed, removed the magnetic bands she didn't need with clothes on, and exited feeling worn around the edges. Her face ached and swelled in places, the skin tight and uncomfortable. *Great. I look hideous. Way to stay off the radar.*

Mila returned to the bridge with her head down. She didn't want anyone to notice her face. She didn't know how bad it was and regretted not looking in the bathroom.

But then she remembered what she would see and stiffened. Bruises, she could handle, but she'd again forgotten she wouldn't see her own features. How could she keep forgetting? Her eyes misted, but she viciously shoved down the emotion threatening to choke her. She didn't need this. She had enough on her plate.

"Jeez, what the hell happened to your face?!" Luke screeched as she sat down.

She sighed. "Not now, Luke. And could you please shut up? I'm already freakish. I don't need any extra attention."

"Sorry. That must hurt."

"A bit. It'll heal."

For once, Luke stayed quiet. She turned to him, concern etching his face. He quickly looked away. She twisted her head to the other side, taking in the captain out of her peripheral vision. He seemed... on edge. That couldn't be good.

Luke tried not to stare, but her gaze flitted to May every few seconds. What happened to her? May looked like she'd gone a couple rounds with Ali. She chewed her lip, biting down on it every time she had the urge to speak up.

She told me not to. I'll ask again when we're alone.

But what if she's in danger? Luke's body stiffened at the idea. She cared about May, had from day one. When she first saw May, she saw someone with a secret, someone different. Not different like she was different, but a kindred spirit none-the-less. And kindred spirits needed to stick together.

Tristan barely noticed as the shift change happened around him. His corpse never returned for duty, which either meant his medical officer had been wrong about the time of death, or the killer had been tipped off.

There was another body on his ship.

Damn it.

He ground his jaw, all his muscles tense as he tried to keep his outer veneer calm and professional.

Another one of his men dead, and he could have stopped it. Should have. This was *his* fault.

He took a deep breath and looked up, inspecting the bridge. The pilot, Trace, jerked her head to face forward when she saw him look up. *Guess I didn't do such a good job at hiding my thoughts.*

The guy next to her kept looking at her at rapid intervals. Tristan watched the concern on the man's face and wondered why. What happened? Was there another incident?

"Trace," he called out, making her turn. He sucked in a breath. Bruises and swelling covered one side of her face. He stood and walked to her station, leaning against the console when he arrived. "What happened?"

"Nothing, sir," she said, keeping her eyes on her work.

"And I'm supposed to believe that?"

"You can believe what you want, sir. I can't stop you."

Tristan bristled, but let it slide. He figured she had reason enough to be irritable. "I believe someone assaulted you. Can you identify the attacker?"

She looked at Tristan, fear in her eyes.

"You can identify him, can't you? You should have gone to the security officers."

She returned to her work. "It's nothing, sir."

"Maybe it was nothing to you, but one of your fellow crew mates was killed. It could be the same person. You might be the only one who's seen him."

She looked back, shocked, fear surging through her frame even harder than before.

"I want to help you," he said, touching her arm gently, but she winced anyway. Clearly, more than her face had taken a beating. "Report to med bay after your shift. That's an order, Trace."

She swiveled back to her console. "Yes, sir."

"I can't believe we've got a shifter on board. Lousy, psycho freaks." The security officer adjusted his gun belt as they checked yet another closet. The ship had about a million of them. And that didn't even include the unoccupied bunks. "We'll never find this damn body. You know that, don't you?"

"Well, not with that attitude."

"Hey!" He slammed the door. "I didn't sign up for this duty to rummage through spare storage."

"Actually, you kind of did. Secure and investigate. That's the job."

"Oh, shut up. What's next on the schedule?"

"Cabinet 15-E."

"Come on," he said, his voice echoing his discontent. "The faster we get this done, the faster we can do something useful."

"This *is* useful."

"Whatever."

<hr>

Mila spent the next few hours grinding her teeth over the impending trip to the medical unit. Whoever examined her wounds would probably look on her with pity. Then security would grill her trying to figure out who attacked her. She couldn't decide which she looked forward to more.

"Ships approaching! Fast!"

"Where?" Mila shouted back.

"Man the guns!" the captain barked.

People scrambled behind Mila, but she was in her element. The tension of her attack, of losing May, of living a lie, it all fell away, leaving just *her*. She monitored her screens, her brain processing the officer shouting out coordinates and trajectories at lightning speed, mapping them in 3D space in her head.

Move.

Move.

Move.

She grinned, loving every second as the big monster responded as well as it could to her skillful commands. She did her best to outmaneuver ships a hundred times smaller than this POS and outnumbering them God only knew how many to one. It didn't matter though. As the swirling colors of sub-space made dizzying paintings in the display, she kept moving, kept avoiding.

Her arms flew over the controls. "Fire," repeated in the background, but she ignored it, her hearing focused on a single voice tracking the enemies.

Move.

Move.

Move.

She watched as fighter ships flew out in front of her, felt the shimmy of the ship from a detonation. *Close, but no impact.* She continued avoiding the tiny ships and their attacks at the same time she tried to avoid planets and moons in sub-space. *Not the best time to battle these bozos.*

She contemplated dropping out of sub-space but nixed it. They had the maneuverability advantage whether in sub-space or real space. If she dropped out, they would only follow her, and she couldn't use her better skill against them.

She was a queen in sub-space. Mila had only done training programs, simulations, but no one ever tested higher. No one could beat her reflexes, her spatial awareness.

Move.

Move.

Move.

As they destroyed the last of the ships, Tristan stared at the back of Trace's head. She was good, damn good. She was, most likely, the best pilot he'd ever seen.

"Damage report."

He continued to ponder as he listened to the various departments reporting back the results of the attack. He vaguely registered there was no serious damage. Between the gunners and her piloting, they'd avoided every major hit.

It didn't make sense. According to her files, May Trace was a mediocre pilot. Barely good enough to receive sub-space travel qualifications. She shouldn't have been able to show off half the moves she just used.

She couldn't be May Trace, not with those skills. Did that mean the real May Trace was dead? His heart sank at the thought.

But that didn't stop him from doing his job. More lay in the balance than a pretty girl with attitude. He motioned to one of the security officers.

"Sir?"

"I want someone watching that pilot at all times."

"You suspect she might be the assassin, sir?"

"Yes."

CHAPTER SEVEN

"That was frickin' awesome, May! You're the bomb!"

Mila rolled her eyes at Luke. "I was just doing my job."

"Yeah and you nailed it. I heard the only damage we incurred was a few low caliber bullet holes."

"Well, that's good."

"Yeah, that was some impressive flying," Santos said as if it physically hurt her.

Mila turned to thank her and noticed two men following them. Following her. "Thanks," she said and spun back forward. *Shit.* She continued on, but felt their gazes on her the entire time. They had security written all over them.

What had she done to attract their ire?

As they entered the room, her shadows backed off, but kept within sight. Mila got her meal and sat with her friends, but remained hyper-vigilant.

I'm dead. I'm so dead.

Her eyes scanned the room as she shoveled food into her mouth, pretending to pay attention to the surrounding conversation.

Her gaze stopped on a man giving her the stink eye. She didn't recognize him, but she *knew* he'd attacked her yesterday.

A hand tapped her shoulder and she shrieked, spinning to meet the new threat.

"May Trace?" the innocuous man said.

"Yes?"

"The captain ordered you to go to the med bay after your shift." He glared at her.

"Busted," Luke said behind her, a grin on his face.

She gave him a glare in response.

"Come with me."

She looked back to the man across the hall who continued to give her the stink eye. She stood and her escorts rose with her. At least she wouldn't be alone.

The examination ended, but she still sat on the bed, the medical officer on a stool in front of her. "Do you have any idea why the man attacked you?"

Maybe. "No."

"We believe the man you described has been dead for several days. A shifter took his identity, an assassin."

"Oh God. Why would he attack me?"

"For new identification, I suspect."

Not likely. "But I thought shifters didn't shift outside their own gender."

"I bed your pardon?"

Shit, information I wasn't supposed to know. She scratched her head, wincing. "I read it. In an article? I mean, it's kind of logic, really. Could you imagine all your junk being different? Gone? Or having extra parts you're not used to? That would give me the willies." She shivered for good effect.

All that was the truth. Shifters didn't like to shift outside their own gender. If you were a woman, you picked female genders, regardless of species. You *could* shift into a male, but it was very unnerving. Mila imagined every shifter had tried it once in their lives, but it wasn't an experience anyone would repeat.

"Hm. Then why did he target you?"

"I don't know. I was mugged about a day before we launched. Do you think that could be related?"

"I don't know. Maybe."

"Well, I can't think of anything else. I'm not a bad person and I try to be nice. I can't imagine someone wanting to hurt me."

He nodded. "Well, be careful. And massage those bruises. It'll help them heal."

"Thank you, sir."

"Alright. Get out of here."

"Thank you, sir."

She walked out into the hall and addressed the security officers. "So, you guys gonna be following me from here on out? Because I'm kind of afraid to be alone."

"Any ideas on who the assassin is now? I was thinking May Trace. Her record lists her as a mediocre pilot, but the skills she's shown are among the best I've ever seen." *And she's suspicious as hell.* Tristan fidgeted in place. He didn't like his crew in danger. With any luck, the other man didn't notice. He needed to *act*, but what could he do?

"No," his head of security said. "She's been acting weird from day one. Whatever is going on with her, it started long before we found the officer dead in the freezer."

"Then who?" And how the hell would they stop him?

CHAPTER EIGHT

*D*ays after the attack, Mila couldn't get back to normal. And her minders both helped and made it worse. She appreciated their presence. Being alone terrified her, but being watched made her want to hide in a hole all over again. Stuck on a ship with hundreds of people, the claustrophobia sometimes got so bad she had trouble breathing. She wanted to escape, run, hide.

But she didn't. Even when her hands shook, even when she couldn't say a word, she continued, trying to appear as if everything was fine.

Certain times were easier. On shift, she could focus on flying. It soothed her, and for a spell, she forgot her paranoia, the attention she didn't want or need.

Same in her room. With only her and Santos, the small space served as a sanctuary. She didn't feel like her heart would pound out of her chest. The darkness helped as well. In the dark, she could imagine there wasn't a wall for hundreds of yards, miles even. It was the perfect illusion, even if she struggled to maintain it. She'd never been good at deluding herself.

Of course, her room had its own perils. She had nightmares, cried herself to sleep, and the darkness could be as bad as the claustrophobia. And every time she woke up from a nightmare, Santos would snap at her to be quiet. She'd never met a bigger bitch in her life…

"May! May Trace!"

"Huh?"

Luke caught up to Mila, puffing and shaking his head. "Jeez, your head's in a cloud lately. What gives? You're stressed, quiet. What's going on?"

"Nothing's going on."

"May, I called you about a half dozen times. How many times did you hear me, huh? And what about your hands? They're shaking half the time."

Mila shook her head. "They're not shaking half the time. Really, Luke."

"They are now."

Mila looked down. The slightest tremble vibrated through them. She clenched her fists, minimizing the shakes. "I'm fine."

"Bullshit."

"Luke."

"Don't even start, May. It may only be the beginning of this tour, but I've got a good bead on you and *this* is not you. So, what gives?"

Mila chewed her lip, contemplating what to tell him. What did she know herself? Not much. "Fine," she said, dragging him into a nearby closet and slamming the door shut.

"Really?" he laughed, the smirk no doubt plastered across his face lost to the darkness of the unlit room.

"Shut up, Luke."

"Well, if I knew this was all it took to get you in a closet, I'd have done it ages ago."

Mila punched him on the arm.

"Ouch."

"Didn't I say shut up?"

"Okay, shutting. I'm shutting up."

She sighed. "I don't know what's happening. What I do know is someone attacked me."

"The day your face looked like an eggplant?"

"Yeah, that," she said, glaring at him, "but earlier too. The day before we departed. I thought it was just a mugging. Now, I'm not so sure. I don't know what it's about, but the captain said there's a murderer on board. And I don't like the scrutiny he and his lieutenant have been giving me. A few days ago, these guys—security, I think—started following me. Constantly. They've done everything short of watch me in the shower."

"Really? Jeez, May."

"Yeah, really." Mila paused, preparing to voice something she'd been resisting herself. "What if they think *I'm* the killer?"

"Oh, May. They couldn't possibly think you're the killer."

"Luke. You don't know that. These people have never worked with me. They don't know me. They've got nothing to go by. I could work as a pilot by day, chop people into teeny pieces by night, and torture puppies on weekends as a special treat. They wouldn't know."

"May, you're getting ridiculous."

The hysteria built inside her, like a volcano ready to blow. "Luke! They're having people follow me! They don't do things like that unless they think you're suspicious. Clearly, they think I'm up to *something*." Her hands shook worse than a palsy sufferer. Her entire being screamed at her to run. She needed out. Now. "I gotta go. I need out of here."

"May, wait!" Luke grabbed her arm, keeping her from escaping. "May." He turned her around, holding onto her shoulders with both hands. "Nothing's gonna happen. I got you. We're friends."

"But my shadows."

"Aren't gonna see anything unusual. You're not doing anything bad on the ship, are you?"

Other than impersonating military personnel. "No."

"Then what's the problem? Just look at them as… bodyguards."

"Yeah?" she said, the shakes calming, her breathing slowing, evening out.

"Yeah. Don't worry. I've got your back. I won't let anything happen to you."

"Thanks, Luke."

"Anytime." He laughed. "Now, let's get out of this closet before you start getting a reputation. I mean, *I'm* fine with it, but you might not be."

Mila punched his arm again. "Very funny, Luke. Let's get to work."

———

Luke rolled her eyes behind May's back. *What a drama queen.* Then again, she supposed after getting attacked and having security dogging her heels, she had a *little* reason to be paranoid. She wanted to hug May, make it all better, but a hug wouldn't fix anything.

And after making that joke about getting a reputation, she was a little uncomfortable giving physical comfort. She'd never dated a girl in her life. Granted, getting caught in a closet might make her seem more normal, but she had a hard enough time maintaining a male persona without trying to fake who turned her on.

<hr>

"This feels like the hundredth closet I've searched." He slammed the door and walked on.

"It probably has been."

"How many guys did the captain assign to this search, anyway?"

"Don't know. I imagine it's quite a few, though."

"And yet we still haven't found anything."

"I talked to Johnson last night. All they've found were two guys doing the horizontal mambo in a closet."

"Okay, I'm glad I'm not Johnson. I don't need to see that."

"See? It could always be worse," his compatriot said with a flourish of his arms.

He flipped him the bird.

<hr>

Mila reached the bridge feeling better. Scared? Sure. Wanting to disappear? Absolutely. But mad with hysteria? Not anymore. She patted Luke on the shoulder, a silent thank you for his words in the closet. He turned and gave her a big grin and a wink. She shook her head. Leave it to Luke to lighten the mood.

She sat down, looking forward to a few relaxing hours at the helm. Strange how wielding true power, the power to shift her body into almost whatever she wanted to, made her feel helpless, alone, and scared. Wielding tens of thousands of tons of steel through sub-space, on the other hand, which required the reflexes of a Jedi Master and most people found terrifying, empowered her, making her feel in control.

As she settled in, she noticed a folded note tucked under one of the controls, keeping it from floating away. *I wonder whom that's from. Not like I have a lot of friends here. Or anywhere, really.* She unfolded the sheet and jumped out of her seat, tripping in her haste. The paper floated in midair as she stumbled back, drawing the attention of the rest of the bridge.

Her heart pounded in her chest, her breaths coming in ragged gasps, as Luke called to her. His voice reached her through a tunnel.

"May? May, what's wrong?" He hurried to her, grasping her shoulder. "May, talk to me."

"Letter," she gasped, whimpered.

Luke turned and snatched the message out of the air before anyone noticed it. He didn't read the note. He just stuffed it in his pocket and returned his attention to Mila. Mila tried to stand up straight, to slow her breathing, but made little progress. She concentrated on calming down as Luke distracted the bridge.

"She thought she saw a bug. Big bug."

Squeals rang through the room. Nobody questioned why Mila still hadn't calmed down.

Parts of the letter echoed in her head. *You are already dead, May Trace. You just don't know it yet.*

She took a final deep breath and straightened. "I'm good. Sorry, sirs."

"You're sure?" the captain said, suspicion in his eyes and voice.

What had he seen?

What did he know?

Why did I ever think this was a good idea?!

CHAPTER NINE

"So, what was in the letter?" Luke asked.

"It was a letter of intent." Mila continued walking.

"A letter of intent?"

"The letter?" She reached out, waiting for him to hand it over.

"Right." He dug in his pocket and pulled out the crumpled mess, slapping it on her palm. "So, what's it say?"

"Let's wait until we're seated and my shadows," she motioned with her head to the two security officers behind her, "are halfway to Neverland."

"Right." He kept quiet about as well as an overeager puppy, but he managed until they sat with food in front of them. "Okay, let's see it."

"See what?" Santos asked from across the table.

"Nothing," Luke squeaked.

"Yeah, because that's not the slightest bit suspicious, Luke." She rolled her eyes.

He sagged. "Sorry."

"I received a rather unpleasant note today."

"Didn't think there was a bug. You don't look the type."

Mila smiled. "Thank you."

Santos shrugged. "So, what's in the letter?"

Luke slapped the surface between them, drawing attention. "That's what I've been trying to drag out of her all day." He would never survive on the lam.

Mila unfolded and smoothed the paper as best she could and laid it out in the middle of the table, holding it down so it didn't float away. She let everyone read silently.

You are quite the foe, May Trace. I've never had to attempt to kill someone twice. Yet I have and you still live. Rest assured, your bodyguards won't save you. I can be anyone. You won't see me coming.

You are already dead, May Trace. You just don't know it yet.

-Your Assassin

"Is he saying what I think he's saying?" Santos looked up at Mila wide-eyed.

"A shifter assassin on board this ship? Holy shit." Luke paled several shades as he fell back in his seat.

"Now you know why I freaked so bad."

"But why does he want to kill you?" Santos pointed at Mila, more interested in her than she'd been the entire tour.

"No clue. I'm-I'm nothing."

"Well, clearly you're something to someone," Santos snarled.

"Well, *I* don't know who that someone is."

Luke sat up. "Seems to me, it doesn't matter who contracted the hit. What matters is catching and stopping this killer."

"Count me out," Santos said, waving her hands in front of her. "No offense. You may be my roommate, but I'm not gonna die for you."

"Thanks, Santos."

"I'm bailing." She stood and walked away, leaving a half-eaten tray behind.

"Well, I've still got your back."

But would you if you knew what I really was?

<hr>

"No worries, May. I'm gonna keep you safe."

Mila peeked over at Luke questioningly for the thousandth time. "No offense, Luke, but you don't exactly seem like prime bodyguard material."

"What, me?" he said in mock shock.

"What kind of hand-to-hand training do you have?"

"Well, I'm a communications officer. What training I have, I probably forgot years ago."

"So, what you're saying is, in a fight, I'd be the one protecting *your* ass?"

"What, a pilot is any better?"

"Yeah, I've been practicing martial arts every day since I was in grade school. I could show you."

"No, no, no," he said, waving his arms in front of his frantic face. "You'd kill me by accident."

Mila shook her head. "I can assure you, I've never killed anyone."

"Good," a voice called from behind Luke.

"Luke, watch out!" Mila screamed, but too late.

A silhouette in the side corridor grabbed and slammed Luke, sending him into the wall using the same maneuver he'd used on her the first time.

"Let him go!" She dashed forward, separating Luke from the assassin to the beat of pounding boots. Years of training kicked in and she blocked, punched, kicked, blocked again, rolled, turned, ducked.

Each move in perfect sync with her attacker's, she did her best, but it wasn't enough. While she'd spent all her time away from people, this man had clearly been testing his skills on his victims.

Someone grabbed her from behind and she yelped, flailing and kicking. One bodyguard raced ahead, plowing into her assailant. He smashed through his enemy's attacks and defenses like a berserker, and before she realized the second shadow held her and not another attacker, their foe ran.

"Go! I've got this," his partner said, the woman the captain had ordered them to follow still flailing in his arms.

"Right." He dashed after the assailant, running with ease, years of training doing him justice. Glimpsing an elbow around a corner up ahead, he picked up speed.

Come on, come on. He reached the corner. A black figure ran a few dozen feet before him. *Damn it.* He pushed himself harder, his feet pounding louder against the flooring, his breaths heaving in and out, powering his forward progress.

The dark shape took a left, but he'd closed the gap, only a dozen feet separating them. He could make out details. In uniform, but not an officer. Nothing on his shoulders. Smallish frame. Five foot nine. He turned the corner.

"Shit." He slid to a halt, darting his head back and forth as he tried to catch a similar build in the crowded corridor. After a few minutes, he picked up his radio. "I've lost him. Canteen."

When she calmed down, the second shadow lowered her to the ground. She trembled from adrenaline, her mind taking in her surroundings for the first time. "Luke!" She dashed and slid to him, laying motionless on the floor.

Someone knelt by her side. "He's alive, Trace, just unconscious."

"Just unconscious?" Her mind tried to dash through a thousand terrible things, but the recent adrenaline surge left it running on neutral. "Shouldn't we take him to med bay? He could be seriously hurt!"

The kneeling shadow pressed his hand to her shoulder. "We've already called someone. They'll arrive with a stretcher to take him there. He'll be fine."

"Right," she said, nodding as a reflex. "He'll be alright?"

"Almost assuredly yes."

She dreaded the "almost" in that statement…

When the stretcher showed up, Mila walked beside it, straining around the bodies of the medical officers to make sure Luke would be all right. She couldn't believe it unless she saw it with her own eyes.

More security officers had arrived and she'd heard one of them order even more to head in the direction her attacker had taken off. *They won't catch him. He's probably already changed his face.* The remaining officers surrounded her on all sides, protecting her like Secret Service protecting the President.

She was too scared and numb to care.

When they finally reached the med bay, a stern doctor practically shoved her onto a bed.

"Sit."

Stay. Lie down. She wasn't sure if her sarcastic thoughts reflected in her face. By now, she wasn't sure she could move her face. The swelling and bruising from her last incident had gone down. She hadn't had the guts to look in the mirror this morning after she'd showered, but it hadn't hurt and it hadn't felt tight. Now she doubted she could smile to save her life, not that she wanted to.

"You took quite a beating, Trace."

"Thanks."

"That wasn't a compliment."

"I'm not stupid."

The doctor palpated her face, his fingers ghosting over her skin, but she winced anyway.

"Sorry."

She nodded and he continued, checking for broken bones. She knew she didn't have any. Shifters left cuts and bruises alone, but you knew when you'd broken a bone. And a shifter could fix a broken bone with no one the wiser.

She winced again as he touched a bruised rib, ignoring the pair of officers still standing guard in the room. She would have complained about the lack of privacy, but she was too tired to care. The adrenaline had definitely worn off.

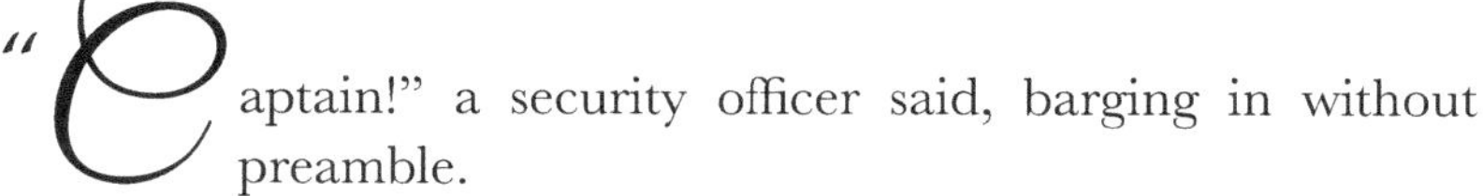

CHAPTER TEN

"Captain!" a security officer said, barging in without preamble.

"Yes?" he said, leaning forward, waiting for the news.

"The assassin's been spotted. He attacked Pilot Trace and Officer Hall."

His heart pounded in his chest in alarm. He jumped up and raced out. "He escaped?"

"Yes, sir. Men are searching for him now."

"Trace and Hall are in the med bay?" His boots hammered the magnetic floor plates.

"Yes, sir," the man said breathlessly beside him.

Three turns and they entered medical at a dead run. He turned and slid to a stop at one of the treatment rooms. Two security officers parted, giving him a clear sight of Trace wearing just pants, boots, and a black sports bra.

He sucked in a breath as he took in the bruises covering her arms, torso, and face. Some, newly formed, turned her skin red and purple. Others had darkened or faded to black, green, and yellow.

He ground his teeth thinking of the pain she must be suffering. *That fucker's gonna die.* He stopped, slackening his jaw and relaxing hands he didn't realize he'd clenched into fists. *Jesus, Tristan, she's just a crew member. And a suspicious one at that. You know nothing about her.*

"Report," he barked, using a commanding tone to reassert control over what must have been a serious testosterone attack.

The man to his left straightened further. "A man came out from around a corner, grabbed Hall, slammed him into a wall. Trace then attacked him before we could get to them. We fought him off and he fled down the same corridor he'd hidden in."

"Any news from the search team?"

"None yet, captain."

"How's Hall?"

"Unconscious, captain. Nothing else to report."

"Have Trace report to my quarters when she's done here." His mind entertained the double meaning there, but he stamped it down before marching off.

"ID." He stood as another in a long line of personnel handed him an ID, which he scanned. He motioned that person to move along, officers behind him directing traffic to a common area.

The next in line stepped up, handing over the ID without being asked. He scanned it and waved him on as well. Other officers were checking each person's private quarters while yet more searched every conceivable hiding place on the Orleans.

After the incident, the captain ordered a full ship lockdown. Anyone on shift stayed put. If you were in your bunk, you stayed there. They were trying to eliminate suspects. They were trying to catch this slippery son of a bitch.

The officer who'd lost the shifter in the crowd had rounded up everyone in the mess hall and galley, which only had one entrance. The man had insisted their foe hadn't escaped. He wasn't so sure.

They had a rough description of the shifter's last alias. Since they didn't think the shifter could create a fake ID on the fly, they searched for anyone who fit the description or didn't have a matching ID. Still, they kept everyone contained, just to be safe.

He scanned another ID as the radio kicked in. "We found another body."

I should have never come here. Oh God, I should have never come here.

Mila dragged her feet. She had no desire to spend any one-on-one time with Captain Faulk. Plus, the more time separated her from the attack, the stiffer her muscles got. Each movement involved jerking her limbs forward like a zombie. And the adrenaline crash made her want to just curl up in the hall for a nap, assassin be damned.

Mila kept forgetting she had guardians. She still had two bodyguards, but not the same two. When did the others take off?

She slowed down even further. What the hell would she tell the captain? Her brain was too sluggish to think, let alone try to deduce what only the real May Trace would have known. Why was an assassin after her?

Mila didn't need the attention. She'd taken May's identity to live her dream. She didn't want or need anyone suspecting her of murder. Anxiety and dread flooded her as her mind obsessed over everyone discovering her secret.

Mila stumbled and one of the guards grabbed her, holding her up. She caught a shared, concerned glance out of her peripheral vision, but didn't care. She just wanted to sleep. Or maybe go back to running, hiding.

They reached a set of double doors and her stomach sank. She couldn't get her legs to move anymore. *Oh God.* One of the shadows opened the door and ushered her in with his arm. Neither of them followed.

Just act normal.

He doesn't know.

Nobody knows.

Through a haze of pain, exhaustion, panic, and dread, the room seemed nice. Big. Especially by the standards of her bunk. As she expected, the place contained no decorations, no personal effects, just the bare bones needed for the space. A desk, chairs. A computer display, but no computer. Computers stayed in the No-Mag room.

Paper records were difficult to manage on a MAG GRAV ship, so there weren't filing cabinets or shelves. Probably, he only kept a few things in drawers in the desk. Cataloging the utilitarian space helped and she felt calmer, more in control. *I can do this.*

"Be with you in a minute," the captain's voice called from one of the other rooms, ramping up her anxiety all over again.

Two doors flanked the office. She focused on trying to identify from which direction his voice had come.

The right. She concentrated, closing her eyes, and heard his feet connect with the floor, coming steadily closer. The door opened and he walked through.

"How are you feeling?" He gestured her toward a chair.

She sat, her muscles shaking, trying to give out on her. Now, she had to stretch her neck back to look him in the eye, which caused her to flinch in pain. "Tired, sir. I just really want to head to my bunk, sir."

"Of course." He sat down on the edge of his desk, still towering over her.

Did he design these chairs to give a height advantage or something?

"Do you have any idea why someone would want to hurt you?"

Mila shook her head, causing a new twinge. She knew a good reason, but no one had that information. Nobody knew she wasn't May Trace, at least not yet.

He frowned. "Since you've been on board this ship, you've acted suspicious. Nervous, out of character. You have a perfect service record and yet I get the distinct impression you have problems with authority. Your record lists you as a mediocre pilot and yet you exhibit skills better than any pilot I've ever seen. You've been attacked twice on my boat, but don't seem to know why anyone would want to hurt you."

Mila's stomach sank, making her feel queasy. Her mouth hung open, shocked, speechless. *What do I do? What do I say?*

He leaned in closer, staring her straight in the eyes. The look he gave her made her want to run. She imagined him using pliers and a blow torch to get the truth out of her.

Mila pressed farther into her seat until the soft cushioning compacted her spine. She whimpered in pain and his eyes softened.

"Could you at least try to fill me in on all you can? Why have you been acting out of character?"

Her thoughts bounced around her head like pinballs, trying to find a way out, trying to figure out how to navigate whatever traps he had in mind. But when she opened her mouth, she just spilled the truth instead.

CHAPTER ELEVEN

"I don't know what's going on. The day before we shipped out, a group of guys mugged me and a friend of mine. I thought it was random. Then I was attacked, then the note, then attacked again."

"What note?" She hadn't mentioned a note before. Maybe they could use it to their advantage.

"Huh?" May looked up, dazed.

"What note?" He softened his voice, trying to coax it out of her.

She shook her head. "Note. Right, sir. There was a note. On my console. Today, sir."

"Can I see it?"

She dug in her pants pocket and pulled out a wad, handing it over to him. The paper had been crumpled into a ball and he tried to smooth it out against his leg. He couldn't remove the crinkles, but he could make out what it said.

He started to read aloud. "You are quite the foe, May Trace. I've never had to attempt to kill someone twice. Yet I have and you still live. Rest assured, your bodyguards won't save you. I can be anyone. You won't see me coming. You are already dead, May Trace. You just don't know it yet. -Your Assassin."

Oh, May. He looked at her in a new light, forgetting her unusual skills at the helm. He felt sorry for her, wanted to help her, protect her. She was terrified and he knew she was no killer. Someone barged in. *Thank God.*

"Captain, a body's been found."

He nodded, back in his element. "Have the two men outside bring her to her bunk."

"Yes, captain."

He looked back at her. "Nothing'll happen to you. I promise you that. I protect my crew." He winced inside saying that, considering they'd just found the body of another of his crew members.

She nodded, and he had to help her out of her seat and out the door. The inevitable adrenaline crash dragged at her, making her moves sluggish. He watched her walk away, feeling a fool for suspecting her. *Of what?*

He turned to the man still standing beside him. "Lead the way."

"What have we got?" he said, a case of déjà vu hitting him as he entered the galley. A corpse lay sprawled across the floor between two prep stations.

"The remains haven't even cooled yet. Fresh, really fresh."

"So, it killed this guy with everyone crammed in the mess hall, one on top of the next?"

"Yes, captain. I suspect as a way of getting a new identity."

"There wasn't anyone in there or the galley without an ID, captain," a security officer with a scanner in his hand said.

Tristan nodded. "Do we still have everyone under wraps?"

"Yes, captain," his head of security, Avery, said. "They're under guard in a common room down the hall."

"Is this guy among them?" He pointed to the corpse.

"No, captain." Avery circled around and knelt by the body. "Our first assumption was that he took on this guy's identity to throw off suspicion, but my men report he's not among those individuals."

Tristan chewed on his lip, thinking. "How many people did you scan?"

The officer with the scanner studied the screen and tapped the display several times. "A hundred and twelve, captain."

"And how many people are in that common room?"

"You think he got away? Right under our noses?" Avery said.

"Maybe. How many?"

Avery touched his radio. "I need a head count in the common room."

Indistinct voices drifted to Tristan. They waited as the medical officer did what he could for the body.

The radio came back to life and Avery nodded, hanging his head. "Hundred and eleven, captain. He got away."

<hr>

Mila dragged herself back to her bunk, keeping her eyes open only by the greatest of efforts. She wanted to just tumble right in bed, but her minders held her back. One officer waited with her while the other entered, checking to make sure it was safe. He exited and nodded.

She locked the door behind her, but didn't get in bed. Facing the top bunk, it might as well have been Mount Everest. She opened her wardrobe, pulled out May's bag, and fished through it, looking for a clue. But her brain refused to kick in gear, so she zipped it back up and collapsed on Santos's bed.

<hr>

"So, what do you want to bet?"

"Bet?" his partner said.

"Yeah, bet. How long do you think it'll be before the captain is doing the dirty with Miss Needs Following?"

"Funny, I thought the captain ordered us to follow her because he suspected her of some wrongdoing, especially considering that first body being found." He tried to pull off a stern, professional, military mien, but his smirk came through.

He elbowed his partner. "Get real. That man is so far in denial, it should be a river."

"Okay, I'll do twenty bucks says a week."

"Twenty bucks? What am I supposed to get with twenty bucks? Grow some balls, man."

"Fine, fifty."

He smiled. "That's better." They slapped hands, but he nodded down the hall when he saw someone coming.

"I see it."

They stiffened and stood tall, watching the figure form in the distance. Female. Tall. At ease.

"Excuse me," she said as she approached.

"I'm sorry. I need to see some ID." He checked the ID. Trace's roommate. Remembering what they were dealing with, he hesitated. The killer could be anyone, including the roommate. He looked to his partner for good measure.

His colleague took up the ball. "I'm gonna have to frisk you, ma'am."

"Frisk me? Are you fucking kidding me? Let me through." She tried to shove past, but they moved in, blocking her way.

"I'm sorry, ma'am. We have our orders."

"This is bullshit," she said while crossing her arms over her chest.

They patted her down, looking for weapons, asking her to take off her shoes. They searched them thoroughly as well. Should they call it in? But the glare she gave them stopped that train of thought and they let her through. Some things just weren't worth it. Weathering a woman's wrath was one of them.

***

She roused to Santos storming around the small space as the last vestiges of her dream faded away. Something about abandoned buildings and cold. Mila groaned as her aches and pains woke up too. Santos zeroed in on her like a heat-seeking missile.

"You," she said, pointing at Mila with death in her eyes. "I can't believe you! What the fuck are you doing in my bunk? And what the fuck's with the psycho commandos outside the door? They tried to frisk me last night when I came back to bed. And they still didn't wanna let me in."

Mila was awake now though she wished she wasn't. Her head thudded from God only knew what, but it didn't distract her from the tight swelling of her face or the stiffness in her abused joints.

"Well?"

Santos's angry rant got the attention of the officers outside. They started pounding on the door. "Trace? Is everything all right in there?"

"Yeah," Mila said, her throat raw. "All's good."

"All is *not* good." Santos turned her back on Mila again, grabbed stuff from her wardrobe, slammed it, and pointed her finger in Mila's face. "If I find you in my bunk again, I'm gonna break you in half."

Mila didn't dignify it with an answer. Besides, what did Santos think she could do that hadn't already been done?

The woman seriously needed to take some anger management classes.

Santos slammed the door, leaving her alone. Mila slid out of bed rather than sitting up and crawled to the wardrobe. She pulled out May's bag again and looked through it in earnest.

She'd taken out things like uniforms, spare boots, and the personal products she'd added to it when she'd taken May's place. There wasn't much left. A powered down tablet, May's toiletries, a USB key, and a metal framed photograph.

The tablet and the USB key were most promising, but she couldn't use either in the bunks. Not sure if the tablet could be turned on safely, she stashed it in the bag and focused on the USB key. That needed a computer interface, so she put it in a zippered pocket of her uniform. She would get her answers after her shift.

CHAPTER TWELVE

Tristan sat at his desk, tracking his guest as he paced his office floor.

"We need to catch this assassin. What is his purpose here?" He stopped, looking to Tristan for answers.

"I've put my entire security force on it. But we're not equipped to capture a shifter. Nobody is." The government had passed a law forcing shifters into camps or prisons. But any shifter worth its salt could escape and evade those hunting it. They had it confined to a ship, for God's sake, but they still couldn't catch it.

Last night, they almost had it. Avery suspected it slipped away with the security personnel, separating out from the rest before they moved them from the mess hall to the common room. The skill this thing had at its disposal was both awe-inspiring and infuriating. The gall! Shifting right in front of his people.

"There's also the attack," Tristan chimed in, distracting his guest from the shifter.

"The attack! At this rate, we'll never get to our destination."

"We will. I told you. I won't fail."

He stared Tristan down, slamming his hands on the metal desk. "The only reason this ship isn't space trash right now is because your pilot had a lucky day. I saw her file. I read all their files. Not a single pilot on this mission should have been able to outmaneuver those ships."

He'd forgotten. Watching her fly through that attack, something didn't add up. She was just *too* good, way too good. How did she do it? Was it luck, as he suggested, or something more?

He stood and focused on the man before him, staring until he squirmed. "Just do your job. I'll do mine." He nodded to him then motioned him to the door.

Mila swallowed hard as she left her bunk. She hadn't bothered to shower today. The idea of getting naked when someone wanted her dead was intolerable. Too much vulnerability. She patted her pocket, reassured by the edges of the drive.

You can do this. You'll be fine. He's already failed twice. She nodded to her guards and headed off to grab a quick snack before her shift.

She missed Luke, who she assumed still loafed about in the med bay. Turning to ask about him, she stopped at the look of pity on their faces. She swung back around and continued down the hall. Maybe she would stop by to see him after eating.

As he went about his protection duty, he felt sorry for Trace. The military bred strong, capable personnel, regardless of their specialization. She should be confident, passing her day without care. Especially with her abilities at the wheel.

Word spread like wildfire. People from the bridge raved over how she handled herself in a crisis, how she maneuvered around the smaller fighters. Many credited her with the minimal damage they took in the attack.

Regardless, he hated seeing how she shuffled through her day, head hanging forward. She grabbed something and ate it while heading to medical. They hung back while she visited with her sleeping friend, Luke Hall, though he overhead the doctor saying that Hall had regained consciousness last night.

Next, she headed to the bridge, again with that listless shuffle. He wondered if her movements were more from her injuries or a broken spirit. She sat in her seat and stared at the station beside her where Hall should have been.

Behind her, the captain never took his eyes off her.

Luke woke up groaning. "What happened?" Rubbing her eyes, she sat up in bed, her brain hesitant to think. Then it all rushed back to her.

Oh, that's the last time I try to act like a dude…

Looking around, her mind still didn't kick into gear. She sighed and leaned against the wall, the noisy environment settling into her consciousness. Then she sat up, her mind alarmed. "Where's May?"

The last she remembered, they'd been walking down the hall together. She never saw it coming. *She* did *protect me in that fight, didn't she?* Luke closed her eyes, shaking her head in dismay. Some protector she turned out to be. "Hello!"

She listened, waiting for a medical officer to show up. What if May was in even worse shape? What if the assassin killed her this time? Her heart tightened in her chest. Suddenly, May's fear and paranoia made perfect sense, because Luke was terrified.

She hadn't been this scared since high school when she decided to live as a girl. She still didn't like looking back on that time. People were cruel. Kids were worse. When she graduated, she decided it wasn't worth it. What was the point in living as a woman if she couldn't pass?

Gripping the sheets tighter, she waited, wondering if she should just slip out of bed and get her answers the hard way.

After her shift, Mila visited Luke again. This time he was awake and perky as ever, sitting up and giving the staff an earful.

"Luke! Glad to see you up and about!"

"Well, not about, but definitely up." He laughed at himself, but his expression darkened as he took in Mila's appearance. "You look like hell. How do you feel? I hope he didn't hurt you too badly."

Mila shrugged. "I'll be okay. I heal quick."

"That's good." But he didn't look relieved. He changed tacks and his smile returned. "The doc says I'll be out of here soon."

"That's great! Glad to hear it. I'm so sorry you got injured because of me."

He waved it off. "Nah, not your fault. Besides, what kind of guy would I be if I let a poor, helpless woman get hurt without at least trying to come to her aid?"

Mila arched an eyebrow at him. "He knocked you unconscious before you even saw him. *I* was the one wailing on him."

"Way to go, girl," he said, slapping her shoulder just hard enough to make her wince.

She healed fast, not that fast.

"Well, I'm gonna go. Get better."

"You too."

She left, guards always a step behind. Now, she just had to lose them.

Giving the security officers the slip wasn't easy. One, because she had no experience at it. And two, because she wanted it to appear unintentional.

Being alone terrified her, but she felt empowered taking some control back of her life. She got a little thrill just thinking about solving the mystery of why someone needed her best friend dead.

She lucked out. They pitied her and people underestimate the objects of their pity. It took a dash of aimless wandering and really good timing, but she caught an elevator just as it closed.

Mila exited onto a hall she didn't recognize. She wandered for a while, feeling sorry for herself and her bodyguards, who she imagined in a panic, calling in backup and a search team. She kept her head down as she made her way through the halls, looking for a computer display.

A few minutes later, she found one and plugged in the USB. She waited for the screen to come out of sleep and covertly kept an eye out for trouble. It seemed to be drawn to her lately.

She selected the file system. Audio and text files filled the drive, all organized by date. She opened the first file, dated a few weeks back and read the screen.

I overheard something today. I didn't see the people, and they didn't say anything threatening or suspicious, but they kept talking about plans and the USS Orleans.

Mila closed the file and opened the next one.

I heard those voices again. Same place, same time. Still didn't see them. I wish I could recognize their voices, but I don't think I've ever met them before. I'm certain they're up to no good.

I considered going to a supervisor, but who? And with what? All I have are suspicions.

One of them is particularly angry. Not a specific kind of anger, just angry at the universe, the kind that bleeds into their personalities until it defines them.

Mila moved on to the next file.

Okay, I'm buying a digital voice recorder tomorrow. I wish I knew where the voices were coming from, but the building is old, and they're coming from the vents. They could be anywhere.

The angry one yelled at the other for "endangering" the cause. I'm not sure I want to know what that means.

The next date was the first with an audio file as well. She opened text file, this one much longer than the earlier entries. May had written notes on her recordings. She'd left the recorder in the vent, then recharged the battery and down-loaded the audio. The entries trailed on and on.

Mila scrolled through the documents in the directory. She clicked the last one, dated the same day May texted Mila.

I've finished going through yesterday's audio and I'm shocked. The anger, the hate. I know their plans now. They're going to sabotage the Orleans.

I don't know what to do. I don't know who to trust. From the sound of their communications, they have a lot of co-conspirators. What if I go to someone and they're in on it?

I have to do something, though. I can't let them succeed. I need advice. I need help. God, I miss Mila. She has a moral compass that always points north. But will she answer my call? I haven't seen her in so long…

Mila closed the document before it went into every little minute detail of May's last day of surveillance. She leaned against the wall, wondering what to do. What *could* she do?

She would look suspicious if she said, "Oh, sorry, Captain. I forgot I'd been running secret surveillance on some yahoos plotting to destroy the ship we're on. Maybe this will help?" But maybe she wouldn't have to.

She scanned through the files again, looking for information. Names, anything that pinpointed the writer. She checked the metadata, but it only listed a branch of the military, not a specific author.

She opened the audio files, listening for her voice somewhere, anywhere. The drive contained hundreds of hours of surveillance. She couldn't listen to it all, but it didn't seem like May used any of the recordings to jot down her own thoughts.

Now she just needed a believable story.

CHAPTER THIRTEEN

Mila gnawed on her lip as she approached, knocked, and waited for the worst.

"Come in."

She eased the door open and peeked inside. "Captain Faulk, sir?"

"Yes, Trace. Can I help you?"

The captain sat at his desk, going over something on his computer display, maybe a shift report. No tension ramped up his form and for the first time since she'd arrived on board, he wasn't giving her an odd look. He seemed… normal.

"I…" She pulled in a deep breath and let it out. "You might want to see this, sir." She walked to his desk, spine straight, and reached out her hand, which held the small USB key.

He took it and plugged it into his display. For a few moments, he scanned through the contents, his expression growing steadily darker. Without conscious thought, she inched backward. By the time he looked up, her back pressed against the double doors, trying and failing to maintain a military at ease posture.

He tried to keep his voice level, calm. "How long have you had this?"

"Uh. Since before we took off, sir. The day before, in fact." She gripped her hands behind her back, her nails digging into her skin.

He stood slowly as he spoke, somewhat calm at first. "You mean to say you've had this the entire time and didn't bother to bring it forward." By the end of the sentence, he was yelling at her.

Mila sputtered, trying to get words out and failing miserably. "I… but… you…"

"Spit it out!" he said as he rounded his desk, coming even closer to Mila.

She whimpered as he came past the chairs on her side of the desk. Within moments, he towered over her. She couldn't look him in the eye. *Just pretend he's not there.* Hard to do when she was staring straight at his chest.

She started blabbering. "I didn't know what it was, sir. A friend gave it to me. I never connected it until now. But after that guy sent me that note and kept trying to kill me? It put the mugging in a new light, so I went through everything I had with me. I found the USB key. It wasn't mine. My friend gave it to me. I swear I didn't know what it was." Tears poured down her face, but she tried to keep her composure, keep it professional, even if she barely remembered what that was anymore. "I swear, captain, I swear. I just wanted to know why someone wanted me dead, sir. I just wanted to know."

Her spine grew straighter as she talked, but she also pressed against the door, defeated and cornered. Still, she tried to maintain her dignity as the captain continued to tower over her.

He sighed. "It's all right. It'll be all right. Who was this friend? What do you know about her?"

"I don't know anything about her. Not anymore. We haven't spoken in years."

He nodded and moved back, giving her space. "I see. Can you summarize the details on the drive?"

She shook her head. "I didn't go over it in any detail. When I realized what was on it, I brought it straight here, sir."

He nodded again. "Good. Very good. What do you know about it then?"

"A conspiracy, sir. She overheard something, a conversation. She knew something was up, so she bought a recorder. Near the end, she realized what was going on, and she texted me out of the blue. She didn't know who to turn to, where to go. She didn't know who to trust. She died that day."

"What?"

"In the mugging. She was killed, sir."

"I'm sorry."

Mila shrugged, even though it cut to the bone thinking of May bleeding out in that alley. "We didn't know each other anymore, sir. I think I mourned what we used to have more than the actual person."

"Any more details?"

"They wanted to sabotage the Orleans, the mission, whatever it is."

The captain nodded.

Mila didn't ask why. She didn't want to know. Above her pay grade.

She started to calm and looked up, realizing the captain was smirking at her. "What, captain?"

"Nothing. I was just wondering. Where are your shadows?"

"I-I… I kind of lost them."

A good-natured laugh spilled from his lips. For the first time, he didn't scare her. He moved back a few steps and sat on the edge of his desk. This time, it didn't feel threatening. It felt normal, lazy, relaxed.

"I imagine you have questions."

"It's none of my business, sir."

"But I think it is. Your life is at risk here."

"I suppose it is, sir."

He sighed. "This ship is on a diplomatic mission."

"A diplomatic mission with whom, sir?"

"With what is more like it," he mumbled. "The US government, along with a slew of other countries from the UN, are initiating treaties with the Incirrina. It's a monumental occasion. It's the first time humans have started negotiations with another species.

"But there are also some factions that have no desire to see humanity peddling to these foreign races. The mission had to be covert. You know how humans can be."

"Yeah, just look what they did to shifters," Mila mumbled, then slapped a hand over her mouth, realizing how inappropriate that comment was.

He didn't even blink. "Exactly. We aren't kind to those we consider different from ourselves."

"So, are you saying you don't hate shifters like most people do?" Mila perked up, looking him straight in the eye, not sure what she hoped for. Hell, she wasn't even sure if she would regret the question and what it might reveal about herself.

"Everyone deserves a chance. I don't believe in blaming someone for the actions of others. For example, if you were a shifter," he said, pointing to her, "I wouldn't blame you, consider you a killer, simply because another shifter on this boat is. You are not it."

"Him," she said as she nodded. "I think I could come to like you, captain." She seriously needed to install a filter on her mouth, though.

"Anyway, back to the discussion at hand. Our governments are initiating these treaties to prevent future conflicts. A lot of alien species travel the stars and not all are as peaceable as the Incirrina. This would ensure the safety of the human race."

"I understand, sir."

"Good, I have to organize a meeting. A lot of people need to know about these developments. Do you mind?" he asked, motioning to the chair in front of his desk.

Mila shook her head, seating herself as she watched the captain set up a meeting, calling people, his head of security, his lieutenant. She waited and after a few minutes, he put down the phone and motioned her to follow him.

"Where we going now?"

"Conference room. I do small meetings here, but too many people need to hear this. They'll never fit."

"Understood, sir."

He pulled open the double doors in a grand gesture you expected to see in movies and marched down the hallway, forcing the shorter Mila into a jog to keep up. They made a couple turns, then he pushed another set of double doors open, walking into a space large enough to fit a few dozen people. Lieutenant Braddock was already setting things up.

The captain walked across the room, motioning her to sit near him. When the lieutenant finished, he sat to the captain's right. When the head of security entered, he sat between her and the captain.

For the next ten minutes, people she had never seen before filed into the conference room, making her increasingly uncomfortable. All of them seemed soft, non-military, about as non-military as she did, only with less attitude. As she watched, she tried to assign traits to them, surmise their roles in life. Then it hit her… they were diplomats. Of course!

Though they wore the station of military crew members, she felt certain they were here to ensure the negotiations this entire mission aimed to achieve. Hiding them among the crew *would* be the perfect way to disguise the ship's purpose.

When the room settled, the captain stood and spoke. "We have some developments. As you know, an assassin plagues this vessel. The bulk of our security force is in pursuit of this felon.

"Through new intelligence I received only moments ago, it has become clear we have a conspiracy against this mission. Multiple people are trying to sabotage this ship and the diplomatic mission she is tasked with. We surmised, based upon new evidence, that that is the reason the assassin is on board. It was sent here to ensure we didn't learn of this plot, which was brought to our attention by Pilot May Trace."

Mila's eyes widened. She shrank back in her seat as all eyes focused on her. *Oh shit.*

"Trace? Would you care to give a report on what you discovered?"

Her wide eyes fixated on the captain who smiled reassuringly at her. She stood and stared a hole in the opposite wall. "I uncovered intelligence regarding verbal correspondence between two parties conspiring against this mission. The audio and text haven't been completely analyzed, but it's clear the Orleans, and this mission, were the intended targets.

"Also, since the one who gathered this information was killed shortly before the ship departed, it's reasonable to assume the two are related. And that the assassin was contracted to keep the plot secret." She looked nervously at everyone around her, then meekly sat.

"Thank you, Trace. Likely the attack a few days ago, which Pilot Trace skillfully outmaneuvered, is also connected. We believe there may be more conspirators on board."

"What?"

"What are you going to do about this?"

"Silence, please. As I said, we are currently sending much of our manpower toward the goal of capturing this assassin. We'll be having a second meeting after this one to plan strategies. Rest assured," he said, staring down most every person at the table, "we will do everything in our power to ensure this mission is a success." Mila noticed that he didn't stare at her or the head of security. What did that mean?

"Now, if you'll all kindly take your leave, we can get to the business of dealing with these new threats."

The room cleared reluctantly. None of the diplomats

seemed willing to leave it at that. Tension grew in the air, the urge to argue the point energizing it. Mila imagined the captain having to deal with them barging into his office at all hours, wasting his time on frivolities.

It took a while, but they all left, leaving only the captain, his lieutenant, the head of security, and Mila.

"Ideas?"

The head of security spoke. "Security's tight. We don't have the manpower for this, not with the current manhunt and security details." He discretely eyed Mila, clearly indicating he disliked the waste of resources on a lowly pilot.

"I agree," the captain said, relaxing back in his seat.

A thought crossed Mila's mind. "Captain?"

"Yes, Trace."

"How did they know where to attack? That just occurred to me. In sub-space, it's hard to pinpoint a target. Almost impossible. It takes advanced mathematics and calculations. It can't be done without a computer. And even then, we don't have to file flight plans like with Earth air travel. We could take millions of routes. So how did they find us?"

"Hm, good question," the head of security said begrudgingly.

Mila shrugged and smiled. "My best guess is someone told. Most likely via TAT. It's the only way to send long range communications. And it would have to be long range.

"It leaves two options. One, a person of no real skill sent a message, loading the message to send to the fleet that attacked us. The problem with that scenario is that the military screens messages randomly. Their plot could be thwarted before it started.

"The second would require a long range communications officer to send a message directly to the fleet. That's a pretty narrow suspect pool. There are only six officers on board."

"Excellent. Great idea, Trace."

"Thank you, captain. We should check the message directory to see which category it falls under."

"Good. Anything else?"

"We could have home base run security checks," Avery said.

"Wouldn't that take too long? I mean, doesn't it take months to run a check? And we're talking hundreds."

"True, but we don't need full reports, only affiliations. Braddock?"

"Yes?"

"I want computer specialists going over that USB key of Trace's with a fine toothed comb."

"I'll be right on it."

"And get more than one person on it. Don't forget there are wolves in our midst. We could very well be sending this information directly to the enemy."

"Of course."

"I'll take care of sending the request to home base," the captain continued.

Mila leaned forward to speak. "You should watch the communications officer as they send it. Make sure they really send it, and unaltered, sir."

"Yes, good, Trace. Thank you. And could you help me with going over the messages in the TAT system?"

"Of course, sir."

"Okay, dismissed."

And boy, did she have no idea what she would be getting herself into.

CHAPTER FOURTEEN

The captain told the head of security, Avery, to continue with the manhunt. He sent Lieutenant Braddock to his office to pick up the USB key while he dragged Mila to the bridge. She followed while her two shadows marched a few feet behind her.

People turned and looked at them as they arrived, surprised to see the captain, no doubt. Most rarely or never saw him. He manned one shift on the bridge while he had subordinates do so on the other two shifts. If something happened while he was off duty, his subordinate would call him.

That was the part she'd never understood about the old space travel shows and movies. It was always the same pilot, same communications officer, same captain. They were always in the same seats. No variation. But systems on board a spaceship had to run twenty-four hours a day. Where were the other shift personnel?

She followed him to the communications console.

"Move," he said, the officers scurrying out of his way. He started typing, his fingers flying over the display, which had an on-screen keyboard. He turned to one of the communications officers who'd fled. "I need this sent back to home base. Now."

"Yes, captain," he said while returning to his seat, where the captain hovered.

She felt sorry for the poor guy. She knew what it was like being on the receiving end of his menacing demeanor. Of course, maybe he was one of the conspirators, in which case, he deserved it.

The captain watched the officer's every move, watched the screen. Nothing would slip by him.

"Good," he turned. "Back to work, everyone. Trace, let's go."

<hr>

The captain had a fondness for grand entrances. Every time he went through a set of double doors, he shoved or pulled them both open. *Dramatic much?*

He walked around his desk and sat. "Have a seat, Trace." Picking up the phone, he said, "IT." After a moment in silence, it connected. "I need a mobile computer display. Yes. Now. Thanks."

They lingered in silence, Mila's gaze drifting over a room she'd absorbed in detail on a previous visit.

The captain broke the silence. "I'm sorry if I've treated you unfairly."

"Sir?" *He's apologizing? Wouldn't have thought him capable.*

"I'm sorry." He rubbed his forehead. "Things have been… challenging, stressful, since this tour began. And, frankly, you're a conundrum. You don't quite act military, which would make me think you would have demerits in your file, but you don't. Your file says you barely qualified for spaceflight and yet you've exhibited some of the best piloting I've ever seen. I just don't get you."

Mila paused, her mind running in circles. "I'm not usually like this, sir. I love flying. It's the only time I feel a semblance of control.

"And my file says I barely qualified because I *did* barely qualify." Mila looked down, trying to pull off embarrassed. "I bombed that test and have been relegated to missions that wouldn't require a great deal of skill. I don't believe I would have been picked for this mission, sir, except no one expected you'd need a decent pilot."

"I suppose that's true." He sat back and stared at Mila, taking her in, maybe trying to piece the puzzle together. *Fat chance. That would be like dumping two puzzles into the same box, then assembling them without a picture.* "Who was your friend?"

"Friend?"

"Yeah, the one who died. In the mugging."

Mila paused, not knowing what to say. She was getting into dangerous waters. Could they verify her story? Or try to? Nobody would find a report of a mugging, but then they didn't know where she'd been when it happened.

"Mila Dragomirov. We were friends as kids. We told each other we would become pilots together. We joined the pilot program but then she disappeared. She left a note. It didn't make any sense. It had contact information. At first, I kept contacting her, hounding her, asking her why. She never answered. I never understood."

It felt good to tell somebody about herself, her story. Even if only a little. Even if she wasn't quite telling the truth.

"Maybe she was a shifter."

She laughed and shook her head. He'd guessed it in one. "Maybe."

Knock, knock.

"Yes?"

"IT, sir. Your display?"

"Come in." He nodded and smiled at her. "Time to get to work."

Mila turned on the display. "What's the directory for TAT message archives?"

The captain got up from his desk and stood behind her, indicating where to go with his finger.

"Thanks." A warm feeling suffused her chest as she gazed up at him, but she ignored it, returning her focus to the screen. "This doesn't… this can't be right. This isn't showing anything further back than a few days ago."

The captain hovered over her shoulder again, his arm reaching out as if to touch the screen, then dropping. "Come on," he said, grabbing her arm. "We're going to IT."

IT was the only place on board with no magnetic floor plates. Because of the computers and servers, it was designated strictly Zero GRAV. Which meant, as soon as you walked in, your feet lifted off and you started to drift.

The room was huge, yet felt tiny. Servers and computer towers were set up in rows, each with grab bars to orient yourself and push off. She grabbed onto the nearest bar, her computer display in the other hand as the captain pushed off in search of a geek.

Though it was usually obvious, this room served as a stark reminder that this ship had no gravity, produced no gravity. Everything, from the foods they ate to the showers and toilets, was designed around that lack. But, when walking down the hall, she found it easy to forget.

Mila smiled. She'd trained to be a pilot, but never been in zero gravity before. She laughed. "This is amazing."

"Trace! Over here."

"Coming!" She pushed off from her grab bar, aiming for the next row, using each one to push her farther. After a half dozen rows, she found the captain holding onto a chair behind a guy plugging away at a computer. "What have we got?"

"It was wiped," IT guy said.

"Can it be retrieved?" the captain asked, breathing down his neck.

"Er, Captain? Maybe give him some room?"

He turned and gave Mila a raised eyebrow, but backed off, giving the man space to work.

Fingers flew across the keys, actual keys, and a few minutes later, he said, "Yeah, maybe. If I..." Another few minutes of key clicking. "Yeah. Yes! Okay. It's not perfect, but we've got some of it."

"Not all?" Mila leaned away from her hold, trying to look the guy in the face.

He turned to her. "Sorry. This person knew to wipe it, but not enough to do a good job. Some data's corrupted, but not everything. It's not perfect, but it's what we got."

"Back it up. External drive," Mila said, paranoia seeming the better part of valor today.

"Yes, go ahead," the captain said. "If they had access to wipe it, they could see the data is back. They could try again and succeed."

The IT guy nodded and went back to his keyboard. He pulled a small drive on a wrist strap off the wall and plugged it in, then they watched as the progress bar filled up.

"Okay, now we can get to work." The captain smiled at her. She should have known that wouldn't bode well.

"What the hell was I thinking when I agreed to help you with this stuff?!" She flinched, forgetting who she was talking to.

"You were thinking it was an order from a superior officer," he said, a smirk on his face.

Mila wanted to break that smirk off, maybe flip him the bird for good measure. She resisted… barely. "How can there possibly be this many messages in the system? We've only been gone a few days."

He nodded. "And there are several hundred crew members on this ship. And shift reports, which each department sends out individually. Even if each person only sent one message so far this voyage that would be hundreds to wade through. With the TAT system, sending messages home is no more complicated than sending an email. And it takes about as much energy to send one message as two hundred."

She faked a smile. "Great. We've been at this for hours. My back feels like a pretzel." She stretched in her seat, her back popping in protest.

He laughed, and Mila wanted to hurt him even more. He stretched as well and she heard his bones and joints popping from across the room.

"I know the feeling," he said as he settled back in his seat. "How bout we take a break, grab a snack, walk around a little?"

"Yes, sir." She was at the door before he'd even stood.

"Eager, are we?"

She turned back to him, and tried not to let it show on her face, tried to remember *some* of her military training. She shook her head. "I don't know how we'll ever find this message. I mean, what if it's in code, sir? What then?"

He walked up to her and grasped her shoulder. "Even in code, some information still needs to come through. Coordinates, for example, or speed and trajectory. Numbers. No matter how it's encrypted, we know what they were sending."

She nodded. "Right, sir. Sorry, sir."

"It's okay. This is long and tedious work. You have every right to be short tempered."

"When are we quitting for the night?" she asked as they passed through the doors. "I have to fly in the morning."

"Don't worry about it. There's an officer in engineering with pilot qualifications. He can take your shift."

"Sir? Wouldn't I be better served flying the ship, especially since you've already said I'm one of the best pilots you've ever seen? We might get attacked again."

"And if we do, my office is only a minute's run from the bridge. I need someone I can trust to sort this out. Otherwise, it won't matter how good your piloting skills are."

She nodded, a little of the tension leaving her body. The captain trusted her. "Right, sir. Okay." She rubbed her hands together. "Short break, then back to work."

"Thank you, Trace."

"It's my job, sir."

"Tristan." He gave her a crooked smile and led the way to the deserted mess hall.

"Ugh, I can barely keep my eyes open." Mila closed out a message and opened the next one. She expected them to blur together soon. Or maybe she would miss something. It didn't help that the messages were a mess. The data was corrupted, all right. Some messages had half the text gone, a bunch of symbols and gobbledygook taking its place.

"Do you want to call it a night?"

Yes. "No. I think I might be to a halfway point soon." *And I really want to catch the sons of bitches trying to kill me.*

"Okay. A bit longer."

She scrolled through the message, closed it out and opened the next one. Most of the messages were boring. Things like, "Hi. How are the kids?" "How's school?" Occasionally, she came across hot stuff, stuff that equated to phone sex. She was just glad home base restricted messages to text.

She exited a message of someone talking to his girlfriend, making plans for when he got back. Opening yet another message, she read, froze, and read it again. "Um, sir?"

"Yeah, May?"

"I think I've got it."

CHAPTER FIFTEEN

Tristan did his hovering thing while she read the message a third time. It listed current position, speed, trajectory, and her name, May's name, May's shift. It said the pilot couldn't evade the attack. "They couldn't send this through home base, could they, sir? And how did they get my file? They had to have gotten my file, right?" But those files were restricted, weren't they?

"Here. Let me." He reached over her shoulder and started tapping the screen. It pulled up an information panel, detailing destination, sender, etc.

The name in the sender category blared out at her. "No." She stood up, knocking into Tristan. She shook her head. "No, he didn't do it. It couldn't be him." The display read, "Sender: Luke Hall."

"I agree. Look again."

Mila looked at the screen in Tristan's hand, then at all the details, trying to see what he'd seen. "The sent period. He wouldn't have been on shift."

He nodded. "And you can't send TAT messages from anywhere but the bridge."

She couldn't help but play devil's advocate. "But what if he posted the message on another console?"

He shook his head. "Those messages are all sent directly to home base."

"Then who was on shift?"

He looked down, checking the time again. "It's around shift change. Could have been any of four people."

"Two, actually."

"Huh?"

"Think about it. The person wiped the directory, but didn't do a good enough job to keep it wiped. So the comp sci people are out. It has to be a mathematician."

"Good thinking."

She smiled. "Anytime, sir."

One of the communications officers sat in a small room on the opposite side of the glass Mila and Tristan stood in front of. He fidgeted and twitched his way along, his gaze bobbing back and forth across the surfaces like a bobble head doll. Avery walked in before them.

"I didn't even know we had interrogation rooms on this ship." Mila looked to the captain.

"Of course we do. This is first and foremost a military vessel. In the past, these rooms have been used for interrogating prisoners of war and enemy combatants."

Mila turned to the smug man sitting in the interrogation room behind them. Each observation room connected to two interrogation rooms. *Efficient.* Mr. Fidget looked suspicious, but she would put money on the guy behind her. She didn't think anyone could sit that cool while waiting to be interrogated by the likes of Avery.

In the opposite room, Avery had started the interrogation. She'd heard his voice rising and falling, but hadn't been listening. The captain was formidable, unnerving. Avery was terrifying. All he needed was a scar running down his face.

Mila glanced at the man behind her again. A small smirk crossed his face. Chills ran down her body. She tugged on the captain's sleeve.

"Yeah?" He turned to her.

"I think Avery's wasting his time. That's the guy." She pointed to the opposite pane of glass. "He's a psycho."

He shook his head. "Psycho doesn't always equate to the right guy for the crime. Where's your display?"

She handed him the flat panel still clutched in her fist.

"Thanks. Let's see this guy's record, eh?" He typed on the screen some, swiped his finger across, then settled on something. "Psycho is probably a good description. The man has more demerits than I thought possible. Why hasn't he been booted yet?"

Mila stretched to see. "There." She pointed. "He might be a psycho, but he's the best mathematician we've got." She pulled her finger across the display. "Good God. Look at all the awards. What's this about a Fields Medal?"

"That's the foremost award for mathematicians. I only know because I've had to screen enough of them as a captain."

"What about the other guy?"

"Hold on." Tristan exited the personnel file and went about finding the other guy's file. "There's not much here. No demerits. No commendations. Nothing. Just ships he's served on, classifications, training."

"Like maybe he didn't want to get noticed."

CHAPTER SIXTEEN

Mila yawned, her eyes tearing up as she swayed in place.

"Oh, I'm sorry, May. Head back to your bunk. Get some rest. I've kept you up too long."

She looked at him critically. "Shouldn't you be doing the same, sir? You've been awake as long as I have. Why aren't you yawning?"

"Just lucky, I guess."

"Well, how about I'll call it quits when you dc, sir?" She might fall asleep on her feet, but she didn't think a captain with sleep deprivation would be much help to anyone.

"Fine, come on. We'll walk you to your bunk."

"Oh, joy," she said, wincing at saying that out loud. She really needed some sleep. "You and my shadows." She slapped her hands together and stretched a worn smile on her face.

"Knock it off, wiseass."

She winked and dashed for the door. "But it's a fine ass, too."

And where the hell did that come from? Sleep deprivation was making her lose her damn mind.

"Sadly, yes," she imagined the captain mutter under his breath.

Yep, definitely her imagination.

When she slipped into her bunk, her roommate slept soundly, just a gently moving lump on the bottom bed. She groaned looking at the ladder to get to hers. Why couldn't she have gotten the lower one?

She contemplated sleeping on the floor, but nixed it as she kicked her shoes into the wardrobe, pulled off her belt, and removed her uniform shirt. In just her pants and undershirt, she slinked to the ladder, collapsing into its rungs and groaning again. The bed seemed so far away.

But she climbed, each rung feeling like a marathon. Three more. Two more. One more. Collapse. She didn't have the energy to tuck herself in. The next morning, she woke with her head propped on her arms and her legs still dangling off the bottom a good two to three feet.

She got up late. Santos was long gone. "Ow." She rolled over and rubbed her shins where they'd pressed against the metal frame all night. She stretched and her back protested with an audible pop. A yawn escaped against her will and she fell back to the bed. *I do not want to get up.*

She slipped down and contemplated a shower. She skipped yesterday, didn't she? Felt like ages ago. She sniffed a pit. *Yep, I stink.*

Damn.

———

After a shower that tormented her with visions of the assassin slipping in and killing her, she grabbed a bagel and headed to Tristan's quarters, knocking on the door.

"Come in."

She peeked in, holding up her breakfast. "Probably should have gotten you one too, huh?"

"Oh, that's okay, May."

"So, what's on the agenda today, sir?"

"Avery's still working on those two suspects, which leaves Comms seriously shorthanded. Hall's the only mathematician trained on the TAT."

"Gotcha. Well, until we figure out who's innocent and who's guilty, there's not much we can do there. How's Luke doing? I kind of didn't check in on him since, well, the USB key thing." She looked at the floor, embarrassed that she'd forgotten about him so easily.

"He's fine. He's working. He's probably wondering where you are right now."

She sucked in a breath. "Oh no! He probably thinks something happened to me. I've gotta go."

"Hey, hey!" He jumped from his seat. "Relax. Don't bother him while he's working, 'kay?"

Mila rolled her eyes. "Like he's working that hard."

He smiled. "Some preliminary background checks came in. Care to help go through them?"

She pulled in a breath and thought of Luke. He would be fine, right? "Okay."

———

Mila yawned. "This would be a whole lot easier in paper. We could just dump them into no and maybe piles."

Tristan looked up from his screen. "You can still do that. Just make folders in the directory."

"It's not the same. This display is a pain in the ass."

He smirked at her. "Get to work, Trace."

"Oh, now we're back to Trace, are we?"

"Well, yeah, when you're slacking."

"I'm not slacking!" But she smiled anyway. Even poring over boring as hell background checks proved entertaining with the captain, which was scary, come to think of it. She didn't want to become attached to anyone, especially him. Not with her problems. How could she get close to someone when there would always be a lie between them?

The floor shook beneath her feet, vibrating the chair under her butt. "What the hell was that?"

Tristan was already standing. "I don't know, but it can't be good."

A klaxon blared and the lights flickered before turning red. *The backup lighting system.* They looked at each other in alarm and ran for the door.

The engines.

CHAPTER SEVENTEEN

They raced through the halls, expecting the worst. The floor continued to rumble beneath their feet. *What the hell is going on?* The captain ran ahead of her, his greater height and longer legs giving him an advantage. Plus, he actually knew the way to the engine room.

Sabotage? An accident? After all, the ship *was* old. It could have just broken down, couldn't it? But her heart told her that was just wishful thinking. No. This was no accident.

They turned a corner and Mila skidded to a halt. A cloud of billowing smoke obscured the path forward. She slogged through it, coughing and holding her sleeve across her face to keep from breathing too much in. People raced past her as her eyes watered and burned. *Where's the captain? I can't see him anymore.*

She stumbled against a hard surface and yelped, flailing her arms and reaching for anything to keep her upright.

"May? Are you okay?"

Good, he was just a few feet ahead of her. "Fine." She

coughed and covered her mouth once more. "Just tripped. Be careful. There's debris on the ground. And I can't see shit through this smoke."

"Maybe you should stay back."

"Not a chance, slick."

"Slick?" She could hear the smile in his voice.

"Get moving, sir."

"Yes, ma'am," he said sarcastically.

They continued on, watching each step, shuffling forward to avoid slamming a leg or foot into debris, to not trip as she had before. Detritus covered every inch of flooring, forcing her to make a circuitous route through the hallway. They still hadn't reached the engine room.

"Shouldn't there be an exhaust fan or something?"

"Yeah. Those systems must be down, too. At least the important stuff is still operational. Actually, I'm surprised the magnetics are still working. They're controlled electronically."

"Right. And they're not vital systems, are they?"

"Nope."

And, as if on cue, she started to float. "Figures."

"Can you touch the wall, May?"

She flailed around and found the grab bars that lined the walls and ceilings of the hallways. At any other time, she gave them no regard, but she whispered a thank you for them now. Her fingers ghosted across one, then she latched on with both hands. "I'm good. Got a hold."

"Good. Let's keep going."

"Okay." She continued, moving arm over arm, afraid to let go with all the smoke. If she lost her grip, she might not find another grab bar in the blinding cloud. She coughed, sucking in more and more smoke, unable to protect her lungs.

"I found the doors. They're mangled. Like they were blasted outward."

"I'm right behind you," she wheezed. A few more movements and she bumped into his flank. "What now?"

"I'm not sure we should enter the engine room with all this smoke. It's huge and I have no idea what's left of it."

"Well, we should at least look." Mila leveraged herself to get ahead of him and held onto the doorway. "I think it's thinning." She squinted through her watering eyes as another bout of hacking coughs plagued her. She scanned around, the smoke shifting toward a few points near the walls. "I think we have depressurization."

"What?!"

"Not major. Small ones. It's clearing the smoke, which is a plus."

"Move over." He nudged Mila aside and looked over her shoulder. "You're right. This could be bad."

"I thought minor leaks weren't a problem."

"They're not, unless something causes them to grow, break open. Then this entire section of the ship would be lost. Hell, the *entire* ship could be lost."

"What do we do?"

"Follow me." And he pushed off.

It took forever for the smoke to clear. Mila floated and watched while men repaired leaks, patching them to regain integrity. She helped by retrieving tools and floating between engineers, but she knew nothing about the engines of the ships she flew.

Then the magnetics reasserted themselves and she screamed as she slammed into the floor.

"May? You all right?" the captain said, racing over to where she'd fallen.

"Fine," she said, getting to her feet. "Just a new cut and a sore bum." She examined the nick on her leg, but dismissed it.

"Let me see."

"You don't have to. It's just a scratch."

"May, please?"

"Fine," she said, sitting down on a large chunk of scrap.

She let him kneel in front of her and raise her pant leg, examining the cut, as she turned her attention to the state of the room. It looked like a war zone. She couldn't recognize anything. Could they recover from this? Was it even possible? She saw nothing that remotely resembled an engine. Just scrap metal.

"How are we ever getting moving again?"

"We will. Don't you worry."

She shook her head. "But this… it's devastating."

He looked around, taking in the damage. "It sure looks that way. But until the engineers assess the damage, we'll have no idea what we're dealing with."

"I suppose that's a better way of looking at it."

"Damn straight. Okay, you should be fine. Just be careful." He tugged her pant leg down and went back to helping get them limping along.

Well, at least the magnetics were operational again.

CHAPTER EIGHTEEN

"Hey, wake up."

"Huh? Wha—?" Mila jerked awake.

"You fell asleep."

She shook her head and looked around the engine room turned scrap yard. "Yeah, guess I did. Any idea on the damage?"

"Come on. Let's get you somewhere more comfortable. We're just in the way here. The best people for the job are already on task."

"Good."

The captain pulled her to her feet, and half carried her back to his office.

"Maybe I shouldn't," she said as he tried to dump her in a chair. "Maybe I should go take a shower."

"Oh, I don't care about the stupid chairs, May. Sit."

He didn't have to ask her twice. She was too tired. Exhausted and grimy. "I think I'm better off flying this POS. Being around you just wipes me out."

He smiled, exhaustion masking his amusement. "It's been another long day, hasn't it?"

"They all seem to be long days lately." She paused, too weary or too empathetic to want to continue. "So, any idea on the prognosis?"

"We're dead in the water. The engineers are hopeful. This is an old ship. The systems are hardier than they seem. They say the damage was done by some parts rupturing. But they think they can weld some of the scrap together, rebuild the engine."

"Impressive." She didn't have the energy to give it the enthusiasm it deserved.

He shrugged. "Sometimes in deep space, you have to be."

"Yeah. How long till we're flying again?"

He shook his head. "That, I don't know. We might never get it running again."

"That would mean we failed, they won."

"Yeah. I don't like it any more than you do."

"What about communications?"

"I haven't checked yet. We've been focused on stabilizing the engine room, making sure we still have life support systems."

"How long will life support last?"

He massaged his face. "Not sure on a rig this old. A few weeks?"

"Long enough for a rescue?"

He nodded. "If we can't get it up and running. And if we have the TAT. You should go. Get some sleep."

"No. I wanna help. We need all hands on deck right now."

"Yeah and you're a pilot with no ship to fly. I think you can afford to get a full night's rest."

"There are other ways I can help, sir."

"Please?"

The exhaustion in his voice made her cave. "Fine. I'll go. But you get some rest, too. You look like you're about to keel over."

"In a little while."

"Soon?"

"Yeah, soon."

A knock came at the door. "Come on in, guys." Lieutenant Braddock and his head of security entered side by side. "Sit. Take a load off."

They both collapsed, more than happy to unwind.

"I'm taking security off the search for the assassin. Our priority now is finding the conspirators. We can't let this get worse."

"I agree," Avery said. "If you want, we can put extra security on Trace." Avery's eyes lit with humor, hinting at something Tristan would not confront head on, especially not with his subordinates.

"I don't think that will be necessary."

"Of course, captain." But the amusement didn't go away. Instead, a smirk appeared.

Tristan refused to acknowledge it. "Lieutenant. You and the rest of the upper ranks. We need to get ahead of this thing. Fast."

"Yes, sir."

"I'll divide tasks out by section. Oversee repairs, everything. Report back to me."

"Yes, sir."

"Avery. May and I have been going over background reports. It's on my private directory. We've divided it out into people who might have unsavory connections and those we found no evidence thereof. I want you to bring these people in, interrogate them. I need answers. Now."

"Yes, sir."

"Dismissed."

<hr>

Emergency lighting tinged every hallway red. Just before reaching his bunk for a much needed nap, four security officers stormed past him. He turned to watch them go, but kept his head down. He didn't need them to notice him, not when success was breaths away.

"Officer Fowler?" one of them said.

He held his breath. Fowler was a friend, an ally. *Be natural. Be normal.* He hunkered down and listened, opening the door to his bunk so he was half in and half out, ready to flee at a moment's notice.

"Yeah? What's going on?" His friend seemed genuinely confused.

Good. That might just save you.

"You're coming with us."

"What? What's going on? What did I do?"

They grabbed him by the arms and dragged him off.

This was only the beginning…

CHAPTER NINETEEN

Mila didn't bother knocking. She shoved the doors to the captain's office open and barged right in.

"Think you own the place now, huh?"

"Oh, I was just trying it out. What's on the agenda today?" She tried to overlook the shadows under his eyes.

"Going over video. I've got most of the ship working on getting various systems back up and running."

"By all means."

"I need a snack. The galley still open?"

"Of course. People need to eat. Even when things get crazy."

"Cool. You want anything?"

"Yeah, just bring me whatever."

She left the room and waited for her shadows to follow her.

They'd been at it for hours. Skimming video of the hours before the explosion, checking camera after camera. The servers and computers shut down during the explosion. They'd had to boot them up again to access the video. They were keeping a single server up while power was at a premium.

Still, they hadn't seen much. They had gone through video of the two hours before the incident which had been officially declared foul play. That was one of the first things they discovered—a simple incendiary device attached to a pipe. Just cleaning chemicals, but they caught fire and heated the fuel, causing weak points in the machines to rupture or explode.

Still, they were looking for the culprit, which meant finding who planted the device. They just had no idea when it was planted, thus hours and hours of video.

"You guys hungry?" she said over her shoulder as she grabbed some quick snacks, snatching them out from under the bands that kept them from floating away.

Neither replied.

She shrugged and started back. *Whatever.*

"Sir! I think I've got it."

He jumped up and moved behind Mila. "Let me see."

She brought it back a few minutes and hit play. This angle showed the pipe where the device would be planted. She couldn't quite see where the bomb would be but the area before it was wide open. A man walked into the frame.

"I don't recognize him, but I don't know a fraction of the

people on this boat." Mila paused it when the man placed the device.

"I don't either. We'll get this to Avery."

Outside his office, the ship felt ominous. They were still on emergency lighting, lending everything a red tint, and the temperature had dropped ten degrees since the incident. Mila jogged beside the captain to get her blood pumping a little faster.

They entered the security offices and the captain shouted, "Avery! Got something to show you."

Avery turned and stalked their way. "Yes, captain?"

"We rummaged through the video. Found this." He handed over Mila's display.

"Great, thank you. It needs to be enhanced. Thanks for the help, captain, Trace."

"Anytime," he said.

Mila just shrugged.

They left the offices, Mila eagerly, not wanting to interfere.

"What are the other pilots doing?"

"Running. The communications systems are mostly down. Can't call people from opposite ends of the ship. TAT's working, but we're keeping it on minimal power just to receive messages from home base."

"Guess I should be glad I got out of that assignment. Of course, if I were running around the ship, I might actually be warm." She started shivering and wished she could shift extra muscle or fat or something.

The captain engulfed her, rubbing her arm vigorously. "Any better?"

"Worlds." *Holy crap.* He felt like a furnace. She wanted to curl up into him and fall asleep.

"Good."

They walked like that, lurching along the hallway, Mila conscious of the looks people gave them. Curiosity. Surprise. Knowing smirks.

But warm trumped all, so she snuggled closer, burying her numb nose in his shirt, which made him laugh.

Then, a loud crack echoed behind her. They spun around in unison. Another crack, and the captain fell to the floor. "Tristan!" Another crack and pain raced through her chest. Mila tried to take a breath, but couldn't. She started coughing, but blood bubbled up, spilling over her lips. She sank to her knees.

A pounding noise faded into the distance. Was that her heart?

CHAPTER TWENTY

The shot cracked against the metal surfaces, hitting him and spinning him into the wall. He fell to the ground, stunned for a moment. Another crack sounded before he'd recovered his senses. He looked up, holding his injured arm as the culprit ran away wearing a security officer's uniform.

The other security officer lay on the floor, likely dead. He continued inspecting the scene. "May!" He half-stumbled, half-crawled to where she knelt, clasping her chest with shaky fingers. "May?" She collapsed as soon as his hands touched her. "Oh God," he said, seeing the terrible wound. A large hole tore through her. He pressed his hand to it, knowing on some level it was too late, but not caring, not willing to admit it.

"Don't you dare die on me, May! Don't you fucking dare!" He didn't feel the tears on his face.

"Someone? Someone help!"

He leaned over her, pressing as hard as he could on her broken chest. "Hold on, May. Hold on."

Her shallow breaths wheezed in, but never seemed to escape again. Blood pooled around his hands, her mouth, the floor. The distress he saw on her face matched his own.

When her eyes closed, he screamed, "No!"

"No, no. May, wake up." He started gently slapping her face, looking for signs she wasn't dead. But she didn't move. He couldn't even see her breathe.

He sat back in shock and waited.

For someone to come?

For a miracle?

He wasn't sure.

But he couldn't leave her.

———

He couldn't look at her. It hurt too much. So he didn't notice when she started breathing again. He nearly screamed when a butterfly touch glanced his shoulder. He spun around and stared gape-mouthed at her. "But you're dead."

May looked down, examining the hole in her shirt with her fingers. He watched in shock as the hole revealed perfect skin, stained with blood but perfect.

"I don't understand."

As her gaze returned to him, the color drained from her face. Fear took over and she started scooting backwards, then trying to get up. But she kept falling. Between the blood-slick floor and recovering from dying, she just couldn't stand.

"May, please."

"I-I can't," she said as she slumped against the opposite wall.

They stared at each other, neither able nor willing to end the silence. His head filled with all the possibilities, all the ramifications. He had no idea what she was thinking.

He felt like he didn't know her at all.

Help eventually arrived and soon medical and security officers swarmed them. Someone was bandaging Tristan's arm while a security officer questioned him.

Mila couldn't stop shaking. She didn't know what to say, so she said nothing. Her gaze kept shifting between the body and Tristan. One because she felt she was to blame for his death, the other because she feared he would be to blame for hers.

She wanted to plead with Tristan not to tell, but he refused to meet her gaze. So she waited, listening to his tale, waiting for the words that would condemn her.

But he didn't say them. In fact, he made no mention of her being hurt at all.

He's covering for me?

"Come on," Tristan said, pulling Mila to her feet. "We're of no further use here."

She nodded, speech still beyond her. She stumbled along, Tristan dragging her behind him by their conjoined hands. He pulled her into his office, dumped her in a chair, and leaned over her.

"What are you?"

The coldness in his voice made her face fall. Her mouth moved, but no words escaped.

He grabbed her chin, looking her straight in the eyes. "What… are… you?"

After several breaths, the truth she'd been hiding forever, the one that could get her killed or worse, slipped out. "Shifter." Nothing more than a breath, he wouldn't have heard it had he not been inches from her lips. It felt like she'd confessed some great sin. Like she'd just admitted to first degree murder.

Tristan stood back, surprised. He shook his head and stumbled, falling in the chair next to her.

After a few minutes of him staring off into the distance, jaw slack, he spoke. "You're Mila, aren't you? Your friend. Dragomirov?"

Mila nodded, numb but also relieved.

I'm not alone anymore.

He sat, contemplating for a moment. "You disappeared because you shifted?"

She nodded again. "Twenty-first birthday. We went out drinking. I got a little too drunk. Drunk enough to do something stupid, not drunk enough to forget." She looked at Tristan, but he wasn't looking at her. "I shifted into a tiger, of all things. I couldn't have picked a dog or something. I can only imagine what the news looked like the next day.

"I managed to get home, shifted back." She paused. "I just packed a bag and left."

"But you left the note for your friend. May Trace." He looked straight at her this time. "If you're here, where the hell is she?"

Mila sagged her head. How many times would the events of

that day torment her before she could move on? "She died. A mugging. Well, maybe it wasn't a mugging. Maybe it was just supposed to look like one." She rubbed her eyes until they hurt.

"You didn't answer my question."

She put her hands down, feeling like she could fall apart at any moment. Like she'd been put together with glue sticks. "I buried her." A tear fell down her cheek. She tried to steel her face, keep more tears from joining it. "Tristan, I…"

He put a hand up. "No. Stop."

"Tristan…"

He looked at her, that same cold expression on his face. "No." He shook his head. "Just give me time, May… Mila. I need time. Space."

"Okay." She stood and headed to the door on shaky legs, too afraid to look back and see that icy visage he'd worn.

When she closed the doors behind her, she ran. She kept running, not knowing if she ran to or away or where her destination would be.

When she arrived, it made perfect sense. The only place on the ship more broken than her… the engine room.

Only a handful of people drifted in and out at the moment. She'd caught it at a lull. Finding a deserted corner, she sat down among the rubble and cried.

CHAPTER TWENTY-ONE

"You know, you've been a real problem for me, Miss Trace."

Mila jumped. She knew that voice. She spun around to confront him and stood slowly. "And that's my problem why?" Her face burned from her tears, but she didn't care. Right that moment, Tristan could be deciding her fate and all because this bastard couldn't leave well enough alone.

"Because I was contracted." He stepped down from the chunk of metal he'd been standing on. "Though I was surprised to find you were a shifter like me."

She shrugged. Would he let it go if she told him she wasn't May Trace? That she was assuming a role, an identity just the same as he?

Doubt it.

"I found a present for you in the galley today when I heard you'd survived." He raised a knife to shoulder level. "I'm good with guns, but I've always been an artiste with knives. It's one of the only ways to kill a shifter."

"I'll keep that in mind." Her stance shifted, balancing her weight, anticipating the strike. She waited, but he just smiled. "Well, are you gonna kill me or what? I mean, you've already tried like four… wait. I've lost count. Not the best assassin, are you?"

Mila grinned when the anger shaded his face.

Perfect. People fuck up when they're angry.

"Aw, did I hurt the little shifter's feelings?"

"Shut up, bitch."

She cocked her head to the side. "Make me."

He charged.

She dodged the first strike, only to get sliced by the next. Her limbs moved sluggishly. *Should have gotten something to eat. I'm running on empty after the gunshot wound.*

Mila pushed his knife hand out of the way and landed a punch to his chin, but he barely responded to it.

Uh oh.

She grabbed his hand, lifting it up, keeping the knife away from her, then slammed his arm into an upright beam. He grunted, but kept his hold. She slammed it again, but her arms were growing weaker, getting cold and tingly from being above her head.

Mila ducked under his arm and ran, knowing the knife wouldn't be able to keep up. She slid behind some debris, crawled under some more.

"You're hiding? After all that bravado?"

His voice grew closer.

She waited. The engine room wasn't deserted, just not packed.

Someone will hear.

Someone will come.

Won't they?

She could feel exhaustion coming over her, a side effect of healing herself.

Someone will come.

"Come out, come out, wherever you are!"

She scrambled farther back, but kicked something in the dark under the scrap metal.

Shit.

"Gotcha."

She slid out and jumped to her feet, registering the assassin's location out of the corner of her eye. She took off at a run again, dodging hurtles, pipes, sharp edges. A piece of piping cut her arm. She bit her lip to keep from crying out as pain lanced across her.

His relentless pursuit seemed in sync with her beating heart.

He grabbed her, whipped her around, and sliced at her throat, but she pulled her head back at the last second, causing the knife to cut shallow. It hurt like hell, but she would survive.

She seized his knife hand with a shaky grip. He yanked out of her grasp with ease, making her stumble, fall. Her head slammed into something hard. *Pain. Black. Pressure.*

The assassin sat on her chest as the pain dulled. He raised his blade. Her half-insensate brain had her grasping for anything, everything. *Cool. Sharp. Grip.*

She sent it up, feeling the cool metal dig and cut into her palm. She screamed as he did, the thing going into his chest under the ribcage, slicing into her hand in three places. Shock covered his face. Metal clattered to the ground. He fell on her, causing her to cry out as the sharp debris in her hand dug in further, pressing on her sternum too.

After a while, when she managed to get the strength, she pushed him off and rolled him onto his back. She straddled him, thrust the chunk of metal a little harder for good measure, not stopping until metal met metal.

He wouldn't recover from that.

Mila stood, staring at her left palm, watching the blood pool in lines. She started to move, but stumbled. Reaching a hand out to steady herself, she screamed when her shredded palm came in contact and collapsed to the floor on her knees.

With a deep breath, she used her other hand to push herself back to her feet. Her eyes felt heavy and she could have fallen asleep right there, but she shook her head and continued.

Mila sensed movement around her, but didn't see. She heard a cacophony, but didn't understand. She just stumbled, walking steadily onward. A humorless laugh erupted from her. She probably looked like a zombie the way she was shambling along.

She collapsed against a wall next to a door she should have known she would run to and knocked three times.

"Come in," the welcome voice said.

She turned the knob, opened the door, and dropped through the doorway, landing on her face.

CHAPTER TWENTY-TWO

*K*nock, knock, knock.

"Come in!" Tristan said. Honestly, why did they bother knocking?

The door opened and a body fell through. "May!" He jumped from his chair, skidding it across the room, and dashed to her side, heart in his throat. "May? God, May."

He turned her over, checking her for wounds. Her throat was slit, her hand was a mess, her arms were cut. *People can't see her like this.*

He dragged her through the doorway, stood and closed the door, then looked back at her, not knowing what to do.

Tend her wounds?

Will she heal herself like she did before?

Should I call a doctor?

He rubbed his face, pacing in a small line next to her.

No one can know about her.

Mila woke in bed. A big bed. A nice bed. She rubbed her eyes, noticing her heavily bandaged left hand. So were her throat and a few choice places on her arms. She blinked her eyes open and turned her head.

Tristan sat on a chair by the bed, watching her. "Hi."

"Hi." He didn't seem as cold as he had before. She almost didn't want to hope as she let the words spill out. "You don't hate me?"

"No, I don't hate you. I just needed time. What I said before was true. I don't blame people for what they are. I blame them for who they are." He shrugged, looking down into his lap. "I don't believe you're a bad person," he paused, "Mila. Mila." A small smile curved one side of his lips. "I don't understand you, but I want to. I know you're not the assassin, and other than stealing someone's identity, I have no evidence you've ever done anything wrong. I would like to know why you did it though."

"Take May's identity, you mean?"

He shook his head, looking down again. "It's the one part I can't get past." He looked up again. "I can't understand it. I wouldn't have done it. I can't imagine anyone good doing it. It doesn't fit with how I see you."

"I didn't exactly have a lot of options, Tristan. I'm a shifter. I couldn't go to the cops and I couldn't just abandon her, the last friend I had in the world. That's why I buried her." She shook her head. "I didn't bury her thinking I would take her identity. I did it thinking I was doing the best I could. Paying her respect.

"When I looked in her bag, I found that she had a verified ID. People don't question verified IDs. I just… wanted a normal life. What I'd been reaching for when my life changed forever."

"When you shifted for the first time."

"Yeah. This was the life I had wanted, that me and May had wanted. We'd wanted it together. It just never happened that way. I thought it was something she would have wanted for me, a gift of sorts."

"What about her family, Mila? When do they get to grieve? Move on?"

Her head sagged. "I didn't think it through that far."

He laughed, shaking his head at her. "Now that *does* sound like how I see you."

She smirked at him. "So, you still don't hate me?"

"No, still don't hate you."

"And you're not going to tell."

"No, I'm not."

Things were getting interesting now. It seemed like victory was within their grasps, but their enemy was dogging their heels too. People were getting taken in left and right for questioning. Some he knew were his compatriots, others weren't. Still, even a blind man could hit a bull's-eye with luck.

He walked the halls still tinged red, rubbing his arms to keep up circulation. Couldn't they turn the heat up a bit? Honestly!

He stopped and knocked at the door he'd been looking for. The door opened, exposing a man in uniform. "I need to talk to you."

The man nodded and ushered him into the room. He closed the door and sat on the lower bunk. "What can I do for you, sir?"

"I'm sorry, but things have reached a boiling point, so to speak." His arms flew out and snapped the man's neck. "I can't have anyone knowing my involvement."

CHAPTER TWENTY-THREE

The security officer sat at a bench, trying to savor the prepackaged snack while he could. Since they'd discovered an assassin on board, he'd been worked half to death. Little reprieves like this never lasted long, often followed by long hours on his feet searching and investigating.

With the temperature plummeting and the ship dead in the water, few people were hanging around. He watched as people walked in, grabbed food, and collapsed on a bench, many times with an exhausted groan. He could empathize.

People rarely stayed long, though. It was too cold to sit still, not without curling up into something like a sleeping bag.

Someone ran into the room, hyperventilating as he bent at the waist. He straightened, but with his breaths coming in gasps, the security officer couldn't make out what the guy was saying.

He stood and walked over to him. "Are you all right? Do you need assistance?"

"Yes." He nodded, the yes more a breath of air than a word. "Found." Another couple breaths. "Body."

"Where?"

<hr />

"Do you mind me asking what happened? How you got cut up?" Tristan relaxed back into the chair as she sat up in his bed.

The words wouldn't come. Looking back, she felt terrified, relieved, nauseous, traumatized, relieved. Her mind kept rebounding to the relieved part. It chewed at her gut, being glad the man was dead, that she'd killed him.

"Mila?"

She shook her head. "You shouldn't call me that."

"But it's your name. Wouldn't you rather me call you by your real name?"

A small smile crossed her face, followed by a wave of nausea. *God, he knows what I am. No one can know what I am.* She struggled to take a deep breath. "Of course, I would, but it's not safe. You'd only be able to use it when we're alone. What if you said it in public? How would you explain that? Huh?"

"I could say it was a pet name."

The smile that crossed his face made her want to smile back, then growl at him.

"What does it mean?"

"I think my parents said it meant 'dear one' in Russian," she said, reluctant to give him the ammunition.

"See? There you go. It's a perfect pet name."

She stared him down. "I still don't think it's a good idea."

"We'll agree to disagree."

"Tristan, this is my life you're playing with here."

His face fell. "I'm sorry."

<hr>

He barged into the captain's office, but for once, the captain wasn't there. "Captain Faulk?"

After a few moments, a door to his left opened and Faulk walked in. "Yes?"

"Another body has been found, sir."

"Shit," he said and sagged before turning and poking his head back through the door. "Stay put."

I wonder who he's entertaining. A muffled reply came through the doorway, but he caught neither the words nor the tone of the message.

"Get some rest," the captain said, before closing the door with a gentle click and facing his new guest. "Lead the way."

<hr>

Mila's eyes bulged as he closed the door on her, jaw slack. *How dare he!* Sure, she'd had a trying day. She was tired and could eat a small bison, but she still couldn't believe he'd just dismissed her like that.

"Damn it," she said as she threw the covers aside. She hadn't gotten around to telling him about the assassin. She'd wanted to tell him, meant to tell him. Mila pulled at her hair as she paced the room several sizes larger than her own.

What'll he think? Will he change his mind about me after knowing what I've done?

Her pacing picked up speed, becoming frantic, her muscles no

140

longer able to keep up. She stopped in the middle of the floor. "I'm getting out of here."

She left Tristan's chambers in favor of her own and slipped into her own bed.

Maybe everything would make more sense after a good night's sleep.

———

Tristan kept pace behind his security officer, but his mind never left Mila. He both damned and praised his job for separating and introducing them. But a ship and its crew comprised more than just one soul and he knew it. He couldn't let his feelings for her hinder him in performing his duties. Too many lives counted on him, especially now.

Tristan didn't pay attention to where he led him, only looking up when they stopped. He slipped effortlessly into captain-mode. "Report."

He hadn't seen a body yet, but his mind kept drifting to the assassin. *Another soul lost to that bastard.* Another security officer approached him, standing up straighter as he neared.

"Captain, he was found by his roommate. Broken neck. Very efficient. Clean."

Tristan nodded, his suspicions confirmed. "The assassin, then?"

"No, sir. We don't believe so."

His head whipped up in surprise. "No? Then who?"

"We don't know, sir."

"Why don't you think it was the assassin?"

"The circumstances don't fit his M.O., sir. For starters, he was left somewhere easily found. Other than once while cornered, the assassin has never left a body in the open.”

“Didn’t you say he was found in his bunk?”

“Yes, sir. But the body was guaranteed to be found post haste. After all, his roommate only had to return to find it. If he was taking on a new identity, he wouldn’t leave it there. Also, the kill is too clean.”

“Too clean?”

“Yes, sir. Military precision. The medical officer says it’s classic special forces.”

“You think it was someone on this ship? Someone who’s supposed to be here?”

“Yes, sir. Perhaps one of the conspirators? Someone trying to cover the trail to himself?”

Tristan shrugged. “It’s as good a guess as any, at the moment.”

Hours later, Tristan finally made it back to his quarters. He sighed, closing the doors behind him. The long day had drained him both physically and emotionally. He thought of Mila sleeping in his bed and a smile crept onto his face. He shook his head and muttered under his breath, “You are a damned fool, Tristan Faulk.”

Tristan walked across the room to his bedroom door, his steps lighter the closer he got to her. Darkness greeted him as he crossed the space and sat on the bed. But his heart sank as he ghosted his hand over the rumpled bedding, massaging the unoccupied space. She’d left. He shivered, the ship’s pervasive chill affecting him for the first time since he found out the truth about her.

CHAPTER TWENTY-FOUR

ristan arrived at Mila's bunk bearing gifts. He knocked and the door opened, exposing a woman he vaguely recognized.

Her face wrinkled into a frown. "Ugh, so not the person I wanted to see first thing in the morning." She opened the door further and pushed him out of her way, heading down the hall without a backward glance.

He stood shocked, floored by the utter lack of respect for a senior officer. "Huh." She disappeared with the slamming of a door and he turned back, knocking once more.

After some shuffling and a crash that caused his heart to jump into his throat and his fist to crush their breakfast, he heard someone stumbling on the other side. The door opened to Mila leaning half-asleep on the doorjamb. "Tristan." A small smile crossed her face and he couldn't help thinking how cute she looked mussed from sleep.

"I brought breakfast," he said, lifting the half-crushed contents to eye level.

"Oh, thank God!" she said, snatching everything before he

could blink. She disappeared into the room, but left the door open.

He took that as an invitation.

The inside mirrored any other bunk on board. Utilitarian, metallic, tiny. She sat on the lower bunk, digging into a beignet. "I still can't believe they have beignets," she said around a wad of dough.

He smirked and tried not to laugh as bits of powdered sugar floated in the air. He wiped a little powder off the corner of her mouth and sat next to her. "I'm glad you like it."

"Like it?" She swallowed and uttered the first clear words this morning. "I love it. God, beignets are amazing. And totally fattening, which is exactly what I need right about now."

"You need fattening foods?" He furrowed his brows.

"No, silly. Calories. I need calories. Fat has over two times as many calories per ounce. After having to heal myself twice yesterday, I need the calories. I feel like my stomach's gonna lead a revolt I'm so hungry."

He did laugh that time. "Well, dig in."

She shoved another beignet in her mouth, again talking around it. "So what happened?" Concern, anxiety, and fear colored her face.

"A body was found in one of the bunks."

"So, not the assassin?"

"No, not the assassin. They think someone else did it."

With a resigned expression, she put her food down. "I should tell you something. I meant to tell you last night, but that guy barged in and I was pretty freaked myself."

The more she talked, the more he realized she was still

unnerved by what happened. He rubbed her arm, trying to soothe her. "You can tell me anything."

She tried to smile, but it looked forced, the only redeeming factor being the dusting of sugar on her face. She looked away and focused on her hands in her lap. "The assassin's dead."

"What?!"

"Last night I ran off, looking for somewhere to hide, somewhere to be alone. I found a corner of the engine room where no one was working and started crying my eyes out." She snuck a peek at him, a self-deprecating look on her face. "He attacked me. I tried to fight, then to hide, run, but I was weak from healing myself. I was tired. He pinned me, but I grabbed hold of a chunk of scrap metal." She gazed down at her hand, tracing with her finger the lines where the metal had sliced deep.

Tristan became more alarmed the longer she spoke. When she said the assassin had her pinned, he nearly came out of his seat. Good God, he'd let that happen. He should have been there. He should have protected her. Instead, he'd sat in his quarters, feeling sorry for himself because she wasn't who he'd thought she'd been.

"I jammed it into his chest." Her words came harder, her voice thicker, like she was holding back a tsunami of emotion. "I killed him." She wouldn't stop looking at her left hand. "I killed him."

Tristan reached for her hand, but she wouldn't budge and he wasn't willing to force her. Instead, he put his arm around her shoulders and pulled her tight to his side. "Shh. No, Mila. You did what you had to. Nothing more. Shh." He rocked her in place.

She started to cry, and a moment's panic flooded him. He froze. *What do I do?* He pulled her into his arms, rocking her again, whispering meaningless platitudes in her ear, hoping some of it, any of it, helped.

––––––––

After a spell, he tucked her into the bottom bed. Kissing her forehead, he watched her fall asleep as he smoothed her hair, wishing they weren't in zero gravity so he could run his fingers through the soft tresses. Mila had long hair, and kept it in tight styles to keep it from floating in all directions, even in sleep.

When his duty finally nagged him into action, he left to deal with the body in the engine room. He stopped to collect Avery and a few of his men, then a medical officer, not that it was needed. They knew what happened and didn't need to investigate.

"What's going on, captain?" Avery asked.

"The assassin is dead."

"Really? You're shitting me!"

Tristan looked at Avery, amused by the man's wording. "Yes, he's really dead, or at least he's been reported dead."

"Who reported it?"

"The one who did the deed." He resisted saying Mila, make that May, had done it. He didn't want to drag her into this mess. She could use a break.

"Look who's being coy!" He slapped Tristan on the back. "Come on! Out with it."

He looked over and shook his head. "Trace. The assassin attacked her again, last night. She almost died."

"Shit, man. Is she okay? I didn't hear about her going to the med bay."

"She didn't. She has a few cuts and I'm thinking the ones on her hand might need stitches, but she's okay."

Avery nodded. "Good. I'm glad. On both accounts."

"Both?"

"Yeah, that the assassin's dead and that Trace is okay."

"Right."

"Do you know how it went down?"

They arrived at the engine room, which was massive and they had no idea where the body lay. Mila hadn't been specific. "Fan out, everybody. It's probably not anywhere that's been actively worked in the last twelve hours or so."

Everyone disbanded, and Avery let Tristan's non-answer slide for the time being. But knowing Avery, that was only a temporary reprieve. Tristan didn't want to relive what Mila had been through any more than she did. He couldn't bear hurting her.

After a few minutes of search, someone called out from one of the deepest sections of the engine room. Everyone made their way there. As Tristan got closer to the scene, he started noticing blood, on the floor, on debris. Dark red from drying for hours, the stains made him relive her stumbling into his office covered in blood. His stomach sank, but he pressed on.

He weaved around pipes and more debris and finally reached where everyone had congregated. The man lay on his back, still carrying the face and uniform of a security officer. A large chunk of black metal in the shape of a narrow pyramid jutted out of his chest.

"Good riddance," someone said.

The medical officer kneeled down and checked for a pulse, not that anyone doubted the man's fate.

Avery spoke. "So what happened and where's our hero? Or should I say heroine?"

Tristan swallowed hard. "Trace is sleeping in her bunk. She had a hard day yesterday and I think she deserves the rest."

"Okay," Avery hedged, "so how much do we know about what happened?"

"She came to the engine room to be alone. Since one of her detail turned out to be the assassin and the other was dead, no one remained to watch her. I didn't expect her to just take off like that. Trace told me the assassin attacked her. She tried to fight him off, but was too weak, too tired. She ran, hid, but he found her. He pinned her to the ground. She grasped the weapon which I assume to be a weapon of convenience…"

"Clearly," Avery said, smirking.

"And stabbed him with it."

"Then how'd he end up on his back?" someone asked.

He resisted the urge to snarl at the man… barely. "I don't know. I didn't interrogate the poor woman. She's been through enough."

Before more questions could be asked, Avery came to the rescue. "Once she's fully rested, I'll ask her some informal questions, make sure her statements match the evidence, but that should be the end of that."

Tristan mouthed, "Thank you."

Avery winked and got back to business.

Tristan returned to Mila's door and wondered if he should

knock. *She might still be asleep.* He rose his fist, hesitating inches away as he bit his bottom lip. *Should I?*

Yearning won out over good sense and his knuckles rapped the door. He waited, but didn't have to wait long. Mila opened the door, a smile gracing her face as soon as she saw him.

"Hi," she said.

"Hiya back."

"Come on in." She threw the door wide and did her best to let him pass in the crowded space. "Where'd ya' go?" She turned her back to him, smoothing the lower bed's sheets.

"Taking care of the body."

She spun, alarm on her face when she looked up at his.

He smiled, hoping to reassure her. "Relax. I told them everything you told me. Avery will come by later to collect a more thorough statement, but the case is all but closed."

"Right. Okay." She sat on the smoothed bed, causing the bedding to contour around her, ruining her previous work. She looked up again. "Thanks."

"There's nothing to thank me for, Mila. I was just doing my job."

"Yeah, but your job could have just as easily thrown me under the bus."

He leaned forward, taking her hands. "I would never do that to you. You have my word." *My heart.*

She nodded and he knew she didn't fully believe him, didn't fully trust him. With a life like hers, he imagined trust had to be earned.

He looked over his shoulder, bit his lip, and prayed to be just as invisible as he always felt. He walked over to the console on the bridge. It wasn't his, but with so many people brought in on suspicions of sabotage, hardly anyone remained to man the thing.

He sat and waggled his fingers in the air, feeling at home, more relaxed, with a computer console in front of him. He went through the motions, going through screen displays, selecting the right options, then started typing.

It didn't take him long to finish his message. Looking over his shoulder again, he checked the other consoles. Most were vacant. The engines were dead, so the pilot and navigation officer were utterly useless. Standard communications were down as well so that chair also sat empty. He moved over to the navigation system, pulling up their current coordinates. Then he used it to calculate directions, distance, and time course for the destination he entered.

He returned to his previous seat, information at hand. He rubbed his hands together, praying he did this right. It wasn't his specialty. He selected coordinates, distance, speed, trajectory, and selected a setting that would have the computer err on the side of caution.

He pressed send and smiled, doing a happy dance in his seat.

Soon, it would be time for Take Two.

CHAPTER TWENTY-FIVE

Mila was making her way to the mess hall, a little dejected that Tristan took off to oversee repairs, when Avery stepped into her path.

"Trace," he nodded at her in greeting. "Follow me."

Her gut sank and she had that going-to-the-principal's-office dread as she slinked behind him.

Oh, shit, now what?

Avery ignored her as he walked off, taking a clear route to the security offices.

He won't put me in one of those interrogation rooms, will he?

She lifted her arm, discretely yanking on her braided ponytail, which tended to float out of reach.

He walked in and ushered her into a smaller office before taking a seat behind a desk.

"This is your office?"

"Yes, have a seat."

She sat, nervous energy revving up her fight-or-flight instinct, but at least she didn't think she would throw up if he asked the wrong questions.

He tapped the computer display on his desk. *Probably just turned on a voice recorder.*

"I have a few questions about the events surrounding the death of the man we've titled 'the assassin.' Just formalities to close the case. You understand?"

"Okay."

"First, according to the account given by you to Captain Tristan Faulk, 'the assassin' was on top of you when you stabbed him. How did he wind up on his back?"

"I pushed him off me."

He nodded. "Can you go over the events that transpired from beginning to end? I'd like to have it, for the record."

"Of course."

Trace left after her statement, leaving a bad taste in Avery's mouth. He saw the marks. The thin red line on her neck, the deep cuts on her palm. But his gut told him she was hiding something, holding something back. He didn't like it. He'd spent too many years eking out a living pulling truth from people to not spot when someone was keeping secrets.

What was she hiding? Did events not transpire the way she'd claimed? Did she seek out "the assassin" rather than the other way around? Was the dead man even "the assassin"? He didn't know and it pissed him off.

He contemplated investigating her further, but saw a universe of hurt in store for him if he did. The captain fancied the girl and being one of the few people here who outranked him, he could cause him a lot of problems. If pushed to it, the captain could easily ruin his career.

He didn't know if the captain fancied her *that* much, but he sure as hell had no desire to find out.

CHAPTER TWENTY-SIX

 ila had hardly seen Tristan the last few days. He'd spent more and more time overseeing repairs he'd already assigned people to oversee, but she could see how being idle didn't sit well with him. He didn't like being able to do little or nothing and he definitely didn't like his ship sitting in open space collecting dust.

Mila imagined him standing in the engine room, pacing like a mother waiting for a child to get out of surgery. She could empathize. She was going stir crazy herself. Flying calmed her, but she couldn't fly. The engines didn't work.

She stood, needing to move, but her room was too small, the walls closing in on her.

Mila dashed for the door, opening it to Luke with his hand raised, ready to knock.

"May!" He pulled her into a massive hug that squeezed the breath from her lungs.

She patted his back, desperate for relief. Suffocating moments passed before he let go, standing back, and without realizing it, allowing her to suck in a deep breath.

"God, May. Where the hell have you been? I've been so worried about you!"

"Around. I've been busy."

He angled an incredulous look her way. "May, you're a pilot. The engines are down. What the fuck can you do?"

"Been helping with the investigations. Maybe I can't fly right now and I have zero knowledge of the engines, but I can certainly wade through endless documents."

"Sounds terrible," he drawled. "Come on."

He grabbed her arm and yanked her through the door, her hold on it slamming the door closed behind her.

"Luke!"

But he didn't listen as he forged his way through the foot traffic of people milling around rubbing their arms or racing from place to place.

After a few minutes, he let go, dumping her in the mostly deserted mess hall. He led her to the food, collecting his favorites before falling onto a bench and slapping the table, encouraging her to do the same. She sat across from him.

At least I'm not cooped up anymore…

He leaned over the table, instantly oblivious of the food he'd collected. "So, tell me *everything*."

She rolled her eyes. Of course, he wanted gossip.

Mila didn't eat anything with Luke. She was too busy filling him in on all the juicy details. So she grabbed a couple lunches and headed to the engine room. She would lay money on finding Tristan there.

When she entered the room, her gaze zeroed in on him. He stood tall, hands on his hips, watching over the repairs. She walked up to him and tapped him on the shoulder. Turning, he smiled at her surprise appearance.

"Working hard or hardly working?"

"Feels like both."

"I brought lunch." She lifted her selection for him to see.

"Excellent. Why don't we sit over there?" He pointed to an area out of earshot, but still within visual range of everyone.

She nodded and went to sit on some debris. "How's it going?"

"It's coming along. The engineers are hopeful. They say there's a chance they can get the engine operational again."

"That's great. Then I'll have a job again."

"Yes, you will."

The next words spilled out of her without her intent, making her want to cover her mouth to keep them in. "I missed you."

Putting down food halfway to his mouth, his lips curled at the corners. "I've missed you, too." He paused, then resumed eating, resolutely chewing before stopping again to speak. "I'm not sure how to do this, Mila."

Do what? She didn't voice it, wanting him to finish, afraid of what he would say. Would he say he didn't want to, couldn't, handle her being a shifter? In her mind, it always came back to that.

Shifter.

Freak.

Monster.

Outlaw.

"I want you, Mila. I like you. But I don't know how to have a shipboard romance, or a relationship with a subordinate. And with everything going on, this should be the last thing on my mind, but it's not. I think about you most of the time."

"It'll either work out or it doesn't. No use worrying about it."

He nodded and they lapsed into silence.

Of course, he knew her secret, which made the stakes much higher.

Too high.

<hr>

A klaxon went off, causing Mila to cover her ears, her heart pounding in her throat. It blared three times, then paused, then repeated. Tristan jumped up, grabbed her hand, and dragged her to her feet.

"Come on." Authority, and a twinge of fear, colored his words.

Mila tried to keep pace as he flew through the ship. It didn't take long for her to realize they were heading for the bridge. "What's going on?" she asked between breaths.

"Imminent attack."

"What? I don't understand."

"Comms were down, are down. We needed a warning system. Three notes means imminent attack."

"Who signaled it? I thought it was an automated system."

"We tweaked it, wired it to the radar console. And a few other places."

She nodded, but he didn't see. She couldn't keep up with him and several feet now separated them. Her heart pounded, but a smile also crossed her face. *Oh, we're so dead.*

She skidded onto the bridge, slightly less graceful than Tristan, who immediately started barking orders. She ran to the pilot's chair, testing the systems, looking, hoping.

They had sub-space, but no propulsion. "Do we have weapons?" She looked over her shoulder. No one sat at the weapons consoles, so no. *Shit.* "Can we get propulsion? Any propulsion?"

"Engineers are working on it. They'll do what they can. They know the drill," Tristan said.

Good thing, because she didn't.

She sat, waiting, her fingers twitching over the controls, her breath shaking with the need to do something, anything. She tested propulsion again. Nothing. "How far out?"

"Couple minutes based on current speeds."

Mila nodded, crossing her fingers the engineers could manage a miracle.

CHAPTER TWENTY-SEVEN

ila felt a rumble and hoped it wasn't the engine room blowing up again. She checked. "Yes!" She dropped the ship into sub-space, watching as it distorted everything around her, bouncing in her seat.

Come on.

Mila urged the ship to crawl forward, not wanting to overtax the engines. She feared what would happen if she did what her entire body was screaming to do. "How close now?"

"Almost visual range, ma'am."

Mila looked around and smiled, seeing their salvation at the same time she caught sight of the first ships in her periphery. She slowly increased speed, steering the ship toward her destination. She watched as the ships got closer, closer. When would they be within firing range?

"Trace? What are you doing?" Tristan said, anxiety in his voice.

"Something they can't."

She felt a small shudder in the controls and someone said, "Impact." She picked up speed.

"May Trace, what the hell do you think you're doing? Those are gas-rings."

"And they're too small to survive gas-rings, captain. We can."

"Don't do this, Trace. The ship's old, has taken substantial damage. We might not survive it either."

"But we definitely won't survive another attack, sir."

She sped up, grinning as Tristan cursed under his breath behind her.

As she approached the gas-rings, visibility decreased. She knew she'd hit them when a large rock smacked into the shield in front of her. Visibility growing worse, she slowed as rocks clanged against their outer hull.

You couldn't avoid rocks in a gas-ring. The gas cloud made visibility all but nothing. The rock and ice from the planet's rings were like land mines in a minefield. You knew they were there, but you had no idea where. All you could do was cross your fingers and pray.

After a few minutes of pinging and clanging noises, she felt confident the POS could manage. It had maintained structural integrity. But now what?

She slowed further, but the controls felt weird for a moment, then a red light gleamed on the console. "Shit." She slammed her hand down. "Goddamn it." She leaned back and sighed. They were dead in the water again.

"M—May. What the hell were you thinking? You could have

gotten us all killed!" Tristan came to his feet, chiding himself for almost calling her Mila.

She turned in her seat and glared. She'd caught that slip.

"If I hadn't done what I did, sir, we'd all be dead. We couldn't outrun those fighters and, like you said, we wouldn't survive the impact. We had a better chance against the gas-rings."

He sputtered, fists locked at his sides, but kept quiet. His jaw clenched as he took in slow breaths, determined to be calm, professional, when he opened his mouth again. "Okay, I need an all systems check. We still have no comms so spread out. Report back here."

"Yes, captain," everyone chorused as they fled the room.

"Not you," he said, teeth still clenched.

Mila sank back in her seat, glaring at him again. "You almost called me Mila. In front of everyone." She waved her hand, indicating those that had already left.

"I know. I'm sorry."

"Sorry isn't good enough," she said as she stood. "I've told you this before, Tristan. You hold my life in your hands." By the time she'd finished speaking, she'd closed the gap between them. "No one can know."

"I know," he said, cupping her cheek.

She raised an eyebrow at him, patting his hand before moving out of his touch. "What should we do? You have them determining the status of the ship. Kind of leaves us with nothing to do."

He smiled. "I could think of a few things."

She shook her head and swatted at him. "Perv."

"Tango leader, please advise."

"Stand by, Tango one. Will inform when a new strategy has been formulated." He closed the comm and resisted the urge to rub his face. Of course, he couldn't. Not with the suit and helmet on.

The ship had been badly damaged. It had already sustained one attack and he saw evidence of further damage on another part of the ship. That pilot had to be crazy to enter a gas-ring. In perfect condition, that ship was too old to enter safely.

Granted, none of their fighters could enter either, even in the best condition. They weren't durable enough, large enough, and certainly were too damned fast. Gas-rings had zero visibility. You couldn't see the obstacles before they hit you, destroying your craft.

At this point, they wouldn't find the ship without a homing beacon.

"Tango unit, flank the gas-ring. I want full coverage. They have to leave some time."

CHAPTER TWENTY-EIGHT

Mila yawned, stretching out at the pilot's console. Why couldn't they have waited for reports in his office? It was a hell of a lot more comfortable.

Tristan had worn a steady path in the center of the bridge from his pacing.

"Would you relax, Tristan?"

"Relax," he said, whirling on her. "You think I should relax? My ship is dead in the water. Again. There is an entire fleet of fighters outside that gas-ring. Again. I'm not sure we can survive long enough to run out of power. Again."

"Relax, Tristan. Or you'll have a heart attack long before any of that happens, or whatever other dastardly fate you've decided we'll meet."

He glared, but it didn't look like his heart was in it. "Sorry."

"No sweat. I get it. These aren't exactly the best of circumstances here. It tends to bring out the best and worst in people."

"It only seems to bring out the best in you."

"And you're any different?"

"Do you think I've handled any of this well?"

"You've done the best you can, the best anyone could have expected." Mila saw movement past him. "I think that's our first report."

<hr>

He waited, listening as his unit continued to report on the quarter hour, reporting back no change. All of a hundred fidgets and gestures had gone through his head as he sat there, but the bulky suit prevented them, driving him half mad with the urge to *do* something.

Then, his console lit up and he touched it, bringing up a map display. A homing beacon.

"Tango unit. Sending you coordinates now. Go to the edge of the gas-ring and disembark. We'll infiltrate in the suits."

CHAPTER TWENTY-NINE

"Brought you food again." Mila waved it under Tristan's nose.

He'd started supervising the repairs in the engine room again. She watched as a swarm of men raced around the room putting things to rights.

"Do you think they can manage?"

"Before? Maybe. Now? Probably not. They'd pieced the engine together before the second attack, but now even more of it's damaged."

"Sorry," she said, her head falling. If only she could have come up with another way. Something, anything.

"It's not your fault," he said, grabbing her shoulder.

Well, that's a change from his earlier assertions. "Still, I feel like I could have done better. Like maybe if I'd stopped sooner, the engines wouldn't have conked out the second time. I don't know."

"You respond well in a crisis, Mila. Don't ever doubt yourself on that front. I wouldn't have wanted anyone else at the helm today."

"Thanks. Now eat."

"Yes, ma'am."

It was slow going through the gas-rings. The suits had limited propulsion, and they had to feel their way blindly around boulders and chunks of ice, using the homing beacon to guide them to their target.

A little farther and he saw his first glimpse of the Orleans since it had disappeared into the gas. Just an outline showed through the thick fog, but he saw it.

Success was within reach.

One of the unfortunate tasks after a strike was checking the outer hull for damage. It couldn't be done from inside the ship when most of her systems were down, which meant someone had to check it visually. Outside.

Him. Him and about a dozen others. He traveled across the surface, tools magnetically clamped to his belt. He found a spot that looked weak, made his way toward it and got in close. *Better safe than sorry.* He pulled out a patch and a tool, and melted the patch in place.

He moved on, looking up around him.

It really was quite beautiful inside a gas-ring. He'd never imagined he might see something like this someday. Sure, he'd expected to have adventures, see the universe, but mostly those had been pipe dreams. It was rare to experience something that struck his heart with wonder like this.

The surrounding space exploded in colors like an aurora, but with the faintest hint of something in it. Depending on the planet, could be ice or rocks. Either could destroy a ship if hit just right.

Still, beautiful.

He furrowed his brow, looking closer at an odd-shaped rock not far off. *It's getting closer.* He squinted, remembering to lift the solar shield. *Definitely, odd shape.* It continued closer, and he wondered what could have set it adrift.

Oh, shit, he thought, as the thing took a recognizable form. Right before the projectile pierced his brain.

He crept to the airlock, reaching for the controls to the left of the door. Fortunately, the ship was old, and lacked any recognizable security measures. He just pressed a few buttons and the outer hatch opened. He went in, waiting for a few of his unit to follow before closing the outer hatch and re-pressurizing.

Air hissed into the room and a light turned from red to green above their heads. He nodded to his men and opened the inner hatch. His men moved out, guns at the ready. Their first priority would be taking out any hostiles quietly. He didn't expect much of the crew to be armed.

Once they were through, he sealed the way out and motioned them to a closet to the right. One dragged a man with him, having snapped his neck. They entered the small room and removed their suits.

"Second wave, ready for entry."

***

She checked the time. He still wasn't back yet. "Hey, John."

A man holding his helmet under his suit-clad arm turned to her. "Yeah, boss?"

"Put your helmet on again. Someone's missing."

"Ah, come on, boss. Max never reports on time. You know that."

"It's not Max. And we're missing a suit, too. Someone's still out there."

He nodded, putting his helmet back on. "Yes, boss."

***

John made his way back from the suit room absently. Turning a corner, he looked up, and dashed back out of sight. "Shit," he hissed. He looked over his shoulder. Nothing should be around that corner. *Think, damn it.* There had been six men. All dressed in uniforms. Not their uniforms, though.

He slipped slowly, and hopefully quietly, back the way he'd come, hoping he could alert someone before it was too late. His suit didn't help. Much more streamlined than the original space suits back in the 20th century, they were still bulky and designed for space. They tended to clomp their way along the flooring, making him curse every step he took.

Clomp, clomp, clomp.

He reached the suit room and pushed the door open, fearing he'd gone too slow, fearing they would shoot him in the back any second. *Come on. Just a bit farther.* He reached the door, opened it, and closed it behind him, leaning against it with a relieved breath.

He removed his helmet and assessed the people in the room. None were armed. "We've got intruders."

CHAPTER THIRTY

*S*ince their uniforms weren't designed for this ship, they'd had to "borrow" from the crew. Not being able to walk, having no leverage to use, could devastate their chances. Even firing guns would drive them helplessly in the opposite direction.

All dressed in the uniform of the USS Orleans, they traveled swiftly, grabbing people and snapping their necks with quick twists. The bodies sagged, then they dragged them to the first available space before moving on. They advanced with precision and determination, like a wave eradicating the ship of vermin.

She slipped out the back of the suit room, grateful for the second exit. Many rooms on this ship didn't have two doors. Most of the men were still removing their suits. They'd told her to run. Bring word to somebody, anybody. Damn, what she wouldn't give for a working comm right now.

She raced on, her mind consumed with the idea that the

people she'd just left behind might already be dead. They had no weapons. They were still in their suits. They couldn't escape.

Why are the corridors so quiet? There's no one here. She passed one crossing after the next, but she encountered no one. Over the last few days, she'd gotten used to people running around like chickens with their heads cut off. Now? When the engines were down and the ship's fate lay in the balance, uncertain? No one.

She turned a corner and bumped into someone. "Oh."

She stepped back, looked up, and *snap*.

"I need a break." The engineer sat, wondering if he could maybe catch a smoke. He'd snuck some cigarettes onto the ship. Technically, they weren't allowed, but he liked to light one up in the airlock, then let the smoke drift out into space once he'd closed the hatch. "I'll be right back."

He had his favorite airlock. Not far from the engine room. He always took a shortcut. Through a back corridor, it emptied out in front of the airlock in question. He rushed, his nerves on edge from too many hours on the job and not enough nicotine. He should have gone on the patch. Then he could have at least not had nicotine withdrawal.

A bit farther and he exited onto the hallway. He walked to the next door, a supply closet. He kept his smokes in there. Best not to keep them anywhere they could be found on a spot inspection of his bunk. He opened the door and a body fell out.

"Fuck!"

Tristan watched, feeling half asleep. Mila had gotten bored a while ago and had been entertaining herself with snacks she'd stuffed in her pants pockets. He found himself fascinated by the plethora of hiding places she'd come up with.

An irate voice shocked him out of his stupor. "No smoking in the engine room! Where the hell did you get that?"

"Oh, fuck off, man. I'm not in the mood."

Tristan looked over at the smoking man and stormed his way.

The man saw him immediately. "Yeah, you were the one I wanted to see."

He didn't sound sarcastic, which gave Tristan pause. "What did you want to see me about? And put that damn cigarette out."

"Not a chance in hell, cap. I need this."

Mila, finally intrigued by events, had reached his side.

"What did you have to say, then?"

"We got trouble. Found a body. And space suits."

CHAPTER THIRTY-ONE

*C*haos erupted as everyone panicked around them, a cacophony filling the room. Tristan barked some word made undecipherable as it echoed off the walls. Everyone quieted, stilled.

"That's better. You, you, and you." He pointed to several people about the room, including Mila. "Come with me. The rest of you, lock this room down. Solder that door shut if you have to. No one gets in until the situation is settled. Do you hear me?"

"Yes, captain." The response rattled off the walls.

Tristan turned and ran.

"Where're we going?"

"Security offices. We need guns."

Mila prayed the entire time, even though her faith had always been a bit lacking. Not really an atheist, her faith had evaporated from disuse. But she prayed now.

There were men on board. Mila imagined them in full body

armor and carrying massive assault rifles. She imagined them shooting everyone on sight.

She shook her head and tried to keep up with Tristan and the rest of them, but she fell behind.

No wonder. Their legs are like a foot longer than mine.

She pushed herself a little harder, wishing she could just add some height or muscle and be done with it, but no. That would probably get her killed. Not worth the risk.

They reached the security offices and she skidded to a halt, slamming into the back of the guy before her.

"Watch it," he growled.

"So-rry," she said under her breath.

She waited to enter, looking in all directions around her, expecting bad guys to jump from the shadows. But there was no one. *Odd.* The others slipped in, allowing her to do so as well. She closed the door with relief.

"Arm up, everyone. Avery. Where's Avery?"

"Here, captain," the head of security said from his office door.

"Set the alarm."

"What for, captain?"

"Intruders. We're under attack."

He nodded and disappeared into his office. After a moment, the alarm went off. A single klaxon repeated over and over again.

"Will everyone know what to do?" she asked, wanting to smack herself for her own stupidity. Of course, they wouldn't. She didn't know. How the hell could anyone else?

"No, but the people who need to will. Let's move out," he said, handing a rifle to Mila.

She looked down at it, wrapping her fingers around the stock.

"You know how to use this?"

Mila shrugged. "Yes and no."

He glared at her. "That's not an answer."

She glared back. "It's not rocket science, Tristan. Sure, I've never used a gun before. Doesn't mean I don't know how."

"Just don't shoot any of my men."

"Scout's honor. I'll only shoot you. How's that?"

***

They marched through the ship, directing everyone they saw to the canteen. It only had one entrance. Large and easily defensible. For now, they had to lock down anywhere the intruders could permanently damage the ship.

"But what if they have explosives?" Mila whispered, keeping time with Tristan's steps beside her. He'd elected to take up the rear with Mila.

"Then we're screwed. Most of our security force is spread out around the ship investigating. Our forces are too thin and my first priority is getting my people safe, getting this ship safe."

The three most vital areas on the ship were the engine room, generator/life support room, and the bridge. They'd split into two groups, each responsible for sealing one of the remaining rooms. Tristan's group was heading to the bridge.

They reached their destination without resistance. Mila let out a relieved breath as Tristan busied himself with locking the controls and the others guarded the door.

"Done!"

He stood and they headed out. All of them exited and Tristan sealed the door.

"Will that stop them?" she asked.

"No, but it'll slow them down. The lock on the consoles should stop them, hopefully. Unless they have a better-than-average code breaker."

"So, what's the plan?"

"Retreat to the mess hall and form one."

***

The room had an air of panic, fear, and pain. Relegated to the fringes, Mila sat back and observed as Tristan, Avery, and Braddock put their heads together to formulate a plan. Her heart thumped in her chest as her senses, heightened from adrenal responses, pulled in every little detail. The tang of nervous sweat, the sharp smell of blood, the wide, shocked eyes, people pacing to keep from going mad, people too afraid to pace.

Chaos. Chaos reigned around her and she looked on it with a morbid fascination. Her surroundings cast a surreal landscape of human panic, distracting her from what lay out there.

She looked back at Tristan, who gave her a smile that couldn't mask the grimace beneath. He went back to his planning, leaving her to her thoughts.

How many are out there?

How many are dead?

Have they gotten into the engine room, the bridge, the generator room?

Can we stop them?

Will we complete our mission?

Will we make it out alive?

CHAPTER THIRTY-TWO

"Tango four, what's your status?" he called over the radio.

"Engine room still secure, sir."

"Well, bust it down, damn it!" he yelled, his voice echoing off the walls. This was taking too damn long.

"We've tried, sir. The doors are soldered shut."

"Well, find something to cut it down."

"On it, sir."

"Tango nine, what's your status?"

"We've breached the bridge, but the controls are locked, sir. We need a hacker."

"Tango eight, report to the bridge." Too damned long. Should have been in and out. Covert infiltration. How the hell did they get spooked?

"Yes, sir."

"Tango twelve, have you found the rest of them?"

"No, sir. Still looking."

"Pick up the pace." He looked up and walked to one of his men kneeling on the floor. "What's the prognosis?"

"No go, sir. We need a cutting tool on this door as well."

"It doesn't look soldered." He looked closer, but saw no evidence of melted metal at the seams.

"It's not, sir. Historically, life support is the most secure room on a ship. Can't risk losing life support and, with it, the entire crew. Door's locked, and from what I remember of this model, there are forty-six bolts holding this door into a reinforced steel frame. It would be easier to go through the wall."

"Well, can we? Is that a feasible option?"

"It would take hours to cut through the wall, sir."

"And the locks can't be hacked?"

The man shook his head. "Once the door bolts are in place, the door can only be opened from the inside. Those locks have no external controls."

He turned and walked away, refusing to vent his bad mood on his men. This was taking too damned long.

"Ready?" Tristan looked out at his men, every security person who made it back, plus Mila and Braddock. He hoped this was the right choice. When discussing it with his men, it seemed logical, smart, essential. But the idea of sending them out against an unknown enemy, with unknown weaponry, training, and numbers, made him ill at ease.

And bringing Mila with them made him even more so, though he suspected Mila would have verbally handed him his balls if he'd suggested she stay behind. She gave him a reassuring smile and cocked her rifle, angling it in her grip like a pro before winking at him with a smirk. He shook his head.

I hope I'm doing the right thing. "Move out."

Avery unlocked the door and men filed out in pairs, taking off in each direction as quiet as mice. Tristan and Mila left last.

"Lock it tight. Don't let anyone in."

The person nodded and he turned to Mila, motioning her to follow him. The door banged shut and she winked at him again before closing her eyes.

"Mila?" he whispered. He wondered why the hell she would close her eyes at a time like this, but then his mouth gaped as she changed. Her musculature got more pronounced and claws extended from her fingers. And he suspected that was only the tip of the iceberg.

She opened her eyes and smirked. Light reflected back and he furrowed his brow.

"Tapetum," she whispered.

"Huh?"

She smiled. "A mirror-like structure at the back of the eye. Reflects light. Boosts night vision."

"Oh. Preparing for battle?"

"You betcha."

"What if someone else sees you?"

"What are they going to see? Only the claws are unequivocal. All the rest? A person could kid themselves into thinking they remembered wrong."

"And you thought it was a risk for me to call you Mila."

"It is a risk. So is this. But I'll risk the possibility of being exposed over the possibility of being dead."

"Of course."

"Now, let's go. We've got some bad guys to beat."

<hr>

"Don't worry. Everything'll be fine," he said, trying to reassure the woman beside him. He'd never seen her before, but many people here had never met before. Well, they said crises were bonding experiences…

"Don't worry? Everything'll be fine?" Her voice escalated on each sentence. "Are you fucking nuts?"

Her voice reached a shrill resonance that made him cover his ears. "Easy, woman. Easy."

"I will *not* take it easy. We are in *shit* here. *Deep* shit. There's a good chance we're never going back home." She burst into tears, mumbling things he couldn't quite understand.

"Do you have family back home?"

She nodded.

"Me too. Two girls." He pulled a photo from a pocket of his uniform to show her. "Couple of hell raisers. Both in college. Costing me a fortune."

She laughed, her tears of a moment ago giving a fragile character to the expression.

"What about you?"

"Newly married," she whispered, her voice so soft he could barely hear.

"That's nice. Wonderful."

She nodded, her eyes cast down at the photograph in his hand as she sniffed. "I'm Tira Santos."

"Nice to meet you, Tira."

Bam.

The room quieted, hearing something slam against the door, metal on metal. All motion ceased as they waited, but for what he had no clue. He imagined not a person breathed in those moments. Tira tensed, staring at the door, ready to bolt.

Bam.

They jumped, the second rap taking them out of their shock. People looked at one another, renewed panic in their eyes.

Bam.

This couldn't be good.

Mila moved like a jungle cat. Graceful, quiet, deadly. Tristan had a hard time pulling his eyes from her as they stalked down the hallways. And so, he kept behind her.

She lifted her hand and they both stopped. Her body slipped to the side in a fluid wave, hugging up to the wall like a cat begging for attention. She slinked against the wall, soundless, coming to the intersection, rifle strapped across her body.

Her hand whipped out around the corner and spun a male form into view. Large red gouges crossed the enemy's face as she lowered him to the ground, dead. She pointed toward the corner, then signaled with three fingers. There were three more.

He nodded, waiting to follow her, rifle at the ready. She turned the corner right before him and flew at the intruders, slamming them up against the wall and onto the floor with speed and precision. He tracked every man she wasn't engaging with his rifle, ready to take him down if he thought for a second he was a danger to her.

He didn't like these tactics, but he understood them. The longer they went without the enemy knowing they were hunting them, the better.

When the last of them lay bleeding on the floor, he dropped his rifle to his side and grabbed a body, dragging it to the nearest doorway. He opened the door and dumped it inside.

"Here," Mila whispered.

He turned and took the radio from her hand. "Good idea." He clipped it to his belt and grabbed the next body.

When they had stowed the last body, Tristan motioned Mila toward a room to the right. She nodded, and they went inside, closing themselves into the darkness.

"Why are we hiding?"

"Because I want to listen to their radio and I don't want to do it while we're hunting. The last thing we need is them tipped off when the radio kicks on."

"But wouldn't they just think it was another of their guys?"

"Maybe. Maybe not. I'd rather not take the chance."

They waited in silence. After a while, Tristan started counting the number of times Mila sighed while waiting.

Thirty-six.

Maybe the team was operating under radio silence. Had they

stopped using the radios once they arrived on board, afraid the signals would be tracked, intercepted? If the enemy was smart, they would.

Thirty-seven.

But then, if they had any inkling how badly damaged the Orleans truly was, they would know it wouldn't matter anyway. Right that moment, they couldn't track shit.

Thirty-eight.

He chuckled to himself and thought Mila might kick his ass if she knew he was laughing at her. But he thought it was cute. She wasn't a patient person.

Thirty-nine.

The radio came to life, a distorted voice echoing off the walls after the dead silence. "Tango leader, this is Tango twelve. We've found the stragglers."

Mila's hand grabbed onto his thigh, holding on for dear life. He tried to look at her in the darkness, but saw nothing. Reaching out, he grabbed her hand and squeezed gently.

"Tango twelve, how many have you got?"

"Unclear, sir. They're holed up in what we assume is the mess hall. Door's locked, but we think we can breach."

Mila's grip tightened, this time claws digging into his leg. He patted her hand, trying to signal her to loosen up, to let go.

"Good."

Tristan crossed his fingers, hoping to hear more as he grimaced under Mila's herculean grip.

"Teams, report in with a status update."

Yes!

"Tango four. We've found a cutting tool. Working on the engine room now."

"ETA?"

"Unclear, sir."

Where the hell did they find a cutting tool? All the tools should have been in the engine room.

"Tango nine?"

"We're working on the data encryption, but Tango eight says the encryptions are much newer than this ship. It'll take a while."

They waited in silence, but no other news came through.

"I guess they haven't found the life support room," Mila said.

"Or their leader is overseeing that part of the operation and doesn't need an update."

Forty.

"Care to let go of my leg, love?"

"Sorry!" she squeaked, releasing her death grip.

His leg started to throb around the sharp pain of the punctures. "Come on. Let's go."

They left the room and Mila sucked in a breath as soon as they had better lighting. "Oh, I'm so sorry. How bad does it hurt?"

Tristan smiled. "Not so bad." He rubbed the spot, eyeing the small red dots that speckled his uniform leg. At least they weren't bleeding.

"Where to first?"

He tapped his fingers against his leg, thinking. It would take hours for them to breach the engine room or break the encryptions on the bridge. The door to the life support room was the most secure. "Back to the mess hall."

Mila nodded and they retraced their steps back the way they'd come.

CHAPTER THIRTY-THREE

The sounds outside the door only grew worse, the people inside nervously staring the door down or cowering in corners. Many of them weren't combat trained. None of them had weapons.

Then the noises outside the door grew to a frenzy, pounding, slamming, cracks of gunfire, screams. Silence.

A collective stillness overcame the room. Was it over? Were they safe? What happened to the men outside the room?

And what made them scream like that?

<hr>

"Where to next?" Mila asked as she dragged the last body out of sight. She scanned the hallway, but she couldn't wipe away all traces of what had occurred with nothing more than a dragged body. Blood smeared the walls, the floor. Droplets of the red fluid hung in the air, creating an eerie tableau, playing silent tribute to the carnage.

Mila found herself oddly fascinated by the drops, wanting to touch them like she had bubbles as a kid. She raised her hand to it, but resisted the urge to touch.

"Engine room."

She turned and nodded, giving one final, mournful glance at the spectacle behind her. "Coming."

Progress was slow through the halls. They couldn't afford to be detected. At each intersection, Mila slowed, listened. With how much she'd heightened her senses, she could pick up a heartbeat at a hundred yards. Still, sound carried on the ship and their shoes weren't designed for stealth.

She waved him through yet another intersection. Tristan followed, obeying her every order. Mila smiled to herself, enjoying the reversal of roles. She held her hand up, signaling to stop. Listened, counted. She wiggled five fingers in the air. Five combatants.

From her memory of the area, they were in front of the engine room doors. She heard what sounded like a saw? Several of them paced back and forth, based on the impact of their boots on the flooring, but it was hard to tell how many. One she could only hear by breathing and heartbeat. Lounging? She focused harder. No, seated. That would give them an advantage, a slight one.

She leaned back against the wall, tugging on her hair as she thought. At that distance, she couldn't eliminate the enemy quietly. Were there other, closer, intersections they could use? She motioned to Tristan, ordering him to move away from the corner. He nodded and they retreated, finding their way to a room that offered a small noise barrier.

Yet again, they were in perfect darkness.

"What is it?" Tristan said.

"Is there a hallway that empties out closer?"

"No. That's it."

"Damn." She shook her head. "We're gonna have to use the guns."

Mila nodded to herself and left the room, slipping back to the corner. Her gaze drifted to Tristan, who already had his gun at the ready. She hefted her gun up as well and nodded before mouthing a countdown. Three. Two. One.

They turned the corner in unison like a couple badasses from an action flick. The loud cracks of the rifles echoed off the walls, hurting her sensitive ears. She gritted her teeth as she held the automatic's trigger, sending a spray of bullets down the hallway. Their opponents fell before they could even start in surprise.

The echoing silence was almost as bad. She lowered her rifle to her side, lifting her hand to her temple to rub at the headache growing there. She groaned, closing her eyes against the pain.

"You all right?" Tristan asked, grasping her shoulder.

She nodded and closed her eyes again when the movement sent sharp shock-waves through her brain.

"Headache?"

"Yeah," she whispered, afraid more sound would only make it worse.

"I'm not surprised. This isn't exactly the ideal place to fire a gun. I've got one myself." He walked ahead, tossing the rifle against his shoulder. "Come on. We've got work to do."

She mouthed okay and followed him to dispose of the bodies once again, wondering if there was a point now.

As she stood over the bodies, a radio crackled to life. "What was that? Was that gunfire I heard?"

Tristan reached over and grabbed the radio, bringing it to his mouth. "This is Tango four. We had a confrontation at the engine room. The threat has been neutralized."

They listened with bated breath, the silence filling them with dread.

Finally, the radio squawked once more. "Roger that, Tango four."

It died once more and they let out a collective sigh.

"That was close," Mila said, feeling weak with relief.

He lowered the radio, some small detail nagging at him. Something was wrong.

"Sir?"

He looked up. "Yeah?"

"Is everything all right, sir?"

"I'm not sure. Go check on the engine room."

"Yes, sir." The soldier dashed off, disappearing from sight around the corner.

He looked to the slow but steady progress on the door, then at the radio. Tango four had sounded… odd. Different. Wrong.

CHAPTER THIRTY-FOUR

Mila wondered what the other teams were doing as they reached the bridge. Had any of them confronted intruders? Had they gotten a radio?

The bridge was another strategically problematic place. The door was closed. No element of surprise this time. And the consoles were too far into the room. No hand-to-hand either.

As they got ready to breach, Mila caught movement around the corner, her ears still ringing too badly to hear someone approach. She dropped to a knee and raised her rifle, preparing to fire.

Tristan grabbed the barrel and lifted it quickly, keeping her from firing. She let out a breath and shifted away any traces of visible changes. Avery and Braddock. She flipped them the bird and they smiled back at her before stationing themselves at the other side of the door.

Tristan did the signaling this time. They had no idea how many men stood beyond that door, so Mila was grateful for the added support. She stood and kept her gun at the ready as she waited out Tristan's countdown, following along in her head.

Three. Two. One. Go.

She entered last, the four of them fanning out in a fraction of a second. Once again, the concussions echoed off the walls, making her blink with each sharp pop that accosted her ears.

Bodies fell, but not without a fight.

"Fuck," she said as a bullet slammed into her arm, sending her into the wall at her back. She tried to return fire, but couldn't control the gun with only one good arm, so she retreated to the hallway, praying the others came out unscathed.

The shots continued to echo in her head long after they stopped firing.

"May?" Tristan called from the other room, her ears so messed up she heard it as a whisper. She didn't hear him enter the hall and kneel in front of her.

When did I end up on the floor?

"You're shot." He pulled at her shirt, checking the wound.

"It's fine. It'll heal."

"Easy. You don't have to yell."

She hadn't realized she'd been yelling. She tried for a normal volume this time. "Sorry."

"Is she okay?" Avery said, exiting the bridge.

"Fine," she reiterated. "Perfectly fine. See? Barely bleeding." She poked at it, not bothered by the pain that flared like a good friend at the pressure. "Can we get going? We've still got bad guys to take out. We know there's at least one more group at life support."

"I like her," Avery said with a huge grin on his face.

Braddock glared at him. Well, he would never be a fan of hers. So be it.

She pushed to her feet. "Let's go."

Mila kept to the back now. She wouldn't be much use. Her head was splitting so much she felt like she could barely keep her eyes open. Just walking was giving her a migraine and she'd long gotten rid of the enhanced senses. Even her normal senses were exacerbating it.

And with her arm out of commission, she couldn't fire the gun. She glared at Avery and Braddock. Without them there, she might have been useful. Claws were better than nothing.

She could have also healed her arm if the two bozos hadn't been there. Mila rubbed her wound, digging in until gating cleared her head a little. Better her arm than her head.

Tristan turned toward her, giving her reassuring looks as they headed to the life support room. Hopefully, that was the last of them. How many more could there be?

After the second report of gunfire, he knew they needed to change tactics. He paced the hall, considering his options. Go after the enemy? But he already had men roaming the halls looking for stragglers. Call all his men back to his location? No, if Tango four's report was false, they had a radio now. The enemy could listen in on their communications.

A crack of running feet against the magnetic tiles reached his ear and he turned. The man he'd sent to the engine room rounded the corner and raced up to him. "Sir. They're dead. All of them. I found them in a room near the engine room."

"Then we assume the men on the bridge are also dead."

The man's eyes bulged, but he kept quiet.

He continued his pacing. The situation had gotten out of hand. This would require a decisive action. "Everyone. Stop what you're doing. We're heading back to the airlocks."

CHAPTER THIRTY-FIVE

They reached the corner closest to the life support room and stopped, Tristan giving orders through hand signals. Mila leaned against the wall, ignoring them and pressing even harder into her gunshot wound, causing it to bleed again. She watched as the slow flow of blood stained her sleeve a little more.

They took off as one, guns at the ready, but there were no shots. She pushed off from the wall and snuck her head around the corner. "What's going on?"

"I don't know," Tristan said, turning in a circle as if seeing the scene from all angles would make it make more sense.

"They retreated? Went back to their ships?" Braddock asked hopefully.

"Doubt it," Mila said, swaggering into the hallway behind them. "They probably have something nasty up their sleeves."

"But what could be nastier? These are the three strategic weaknesses of the ship. They haven't managed any of them."

Mila looked up at him, alarmed. "The airlocks. If they can trip the airlocks…"

"Everyone on board would suffocate," he finished.

"But they could be at any of them," Avery chimed in.

"Well, how many are there?" Mila started pacing, thinking.

"Too many for us to cover individually," Tristan said with a sigh.

"Well, do we know which airlock they came from?"

They looked at each other, growing panic setting the mood.

"By the engine room!" Tristan exclaimed. "That's where the suits were found."

"Well, let's go."

They took off, no longer caring about stealth. If they didn't get there in time, everyone would die.

Mila lost ground, not being able to keep up with the longer strides of her companions. Her lungs burned, her legs burned, her arm burned and throbbed, her head throbbed. She felt like her body would conk out at any moment. *Not now!* She tried to concentrate through the haze brought on by her headache. Shifters had unbelievable control over their bodies. Not just changing tissue, which allowed them to heal, but changing how their bodies functioned.

Like right now, she could really use some adrenaline and endorphins. Her head fought her, skull splitting with the pain from abused senses. Mila focused and gradually, her body rewarded her. She sped up as the pain lessened, became manageable.

She still couldn't close the gap, though. Not without doing something noticeable. But she kept on, using the pounding rhythm of their feet as a hypnotic metronome to keep her going almost effortlessly. Her mind cleared for the first time in quite a while.

They had to get to that airlock.

Tristan pointed. The suit room must be up ahead. They angled toward it, but Mila had other plans. She couldn't let the enemy get to that airlock. Suits would only slow them down. The others ran into the suit room, preparing for the inevitable.

She ran straight past and looked back. *Yes!* They didn't notice. She reached the end of the corridor and enhanced her hearing, listening for the enemy. She heard them putting on suits. Not all of them, though. Some must have been playing sentry. She returned her hearing to normal. She didn't want a repeat occurrence if she had to open fire.

Mila prepared herself, taking deep breaths. *Remember. Don't hold your breath. If the airlock opens, don't hold your breath or you'll die. They'll have ninety seconds to rescue you if you don't hold your breath.*

She shifted what she needed. Speed. Strength. Claws. And turned the corner at a dead run. Her feet pounded on the metallic plates. Otherwise, she didn't make a sound, charging like a train on its tracks toward the sentry who turned, raising his weapon. He didn't get to fire as she jumped, landing on his chest and knocking him to the ground, her claws buried between his ribs.

Mila took a fraction of a second, the blink of an eye, to reassess the situation, picking her next target from the movements he made. *That one's lifting a gun.* She charged again, raking her hand across him and throwing him into the wall. After that, each of her movements was fluid, like a ballet, one attack flowing into the next. One man after another went down. Claps of gunfire sounded, but everything missed, her movements too erratic to predict, to follow.

Then, a warning sounded, causing her head to come up. "Oh shit." A single crack of a gun echoed off the walls and the bullet knocked her back, stunning her for a moment. But the bullet meant nothing. The injury meant nothing. The doors were opening.

***

Mila raced to the control panel, ignoring the rest of the enemy who still had weapons and fight in them. *No!* She ran, feeling like a tortoise could run faster. She wouldn't make it. She couldn't make it. She had to make it.

The alarm gained intensity and the light above the door changed from green to red. *No!* She grabbed the man at the console, shoving him from the panel, but it was too late. The doors opened, and she latched onto the first thing in sight as the sharp pressure change caused by the opening tried to equalize the two systems.

Things, bodies, something flew by her as she held on for dear life. It was her life. If she let go, they might not get to her in time. Ninety seconds. In vacuum, she had ninety seconds before permanent damage ensued. She had to hold out, but she could feel her fingers slipping.

Her injured arm felt increasingly weak, unable to keep up even with the adrenaline pumping through her system. *Come on! Just hold on till they get here. All they have to do is close the outer hatch.* Her arm started to go numb, then slipped from the surface. One hand left. *Just hold on.* But black spots were starting to form over her eyes. Her other arm was starting to feel numb. *No! Just a little longer. They'll get to me!*

But that arm too gave up the fight and she sailed into space. *Try to breathe. No air. Try to breathe. Suffocating. Can't think.* She told herself to breathe. Count. How many seconds before she lost consciousness? Nine? Ten? Eleven? Lack of oxygen was making her head fuzzy. How many seconds now?

She couldn't help watching the ship's portal shrink as momentum forced her to drift farther and farther from help.

Sorry, Tristan.

CHAPTER THIRTY-SIX

Tristan ran into the room, racing to the nearest suit, expecting everyone to follow. Bodies dashed around him, stumbling and jumping as they tried to suit up in lightning speed when the suits were not designed to be donned in a rush. He'd zipped up and grabbed a helmet before he turned and realized with monumental dread that Mila wasn't there. "Oh no."

"Captain?" Avery asked.

"She didn't. She did," he said in a daze.

"Captain, what's wrong?" Braddock asked.

"M—," he said before stopping himself again from saying her real name. "May's gone ahead."

"That wasn't the plan!" Avery shouted, forgetting that the enemy was just around the corner.

He looked over. "No shit!" His heart raced even harder than when they'd run down the halls, fearing the worst, fearing they would be too late. Now, he knew he would be too late. For her.

Shots echoed down the hall, spurring them to action. They

waddled for the door, slowed by the suits that might very well save them, save everyone, if those doors opened.

Frustration built as they moved slowly down the hall, serenaded by the song of violence. *As long as those guns are firing, she's still alive.* He took little comfort in the thought.

An alarm sounded. Depressurization warning. "Helmets on! Now!"

They complied as they continued to make slow but steady progress. They would be too late. He just knew it. He couldn't fail her. He couldn't.

A second more strident alarm sounded and he felt the pull as the chamber started depressurizing. *No!* He made the corner, turned and saw Mila, holding onto the control panel with only one arm, her other dangling useless beside her.

He tried to pick up speed, but his progress was slow. *Just hold on.* He watched, breath coming in shallow, pained fits, as her fingers lost their grip. "No!" He reached out, but he still wasn't close enough. She drifted through the hatch and into space.

He jumped, hoping the force of the depressurization was greater than the magnetics. He couldn't engage the propulsion on the suit until he cleared the opening. *Hold on, Mila.*

Avery didn't bother trying to correct his captain, tell him not to chase after her. He had more important things to consider. Like closing that hatch. One life wasn't worth losing the entire ship.

He waddled to the control panel as it became harder and harder to keep his feet on the floor. Fortunately, the soles of the suits were designed to walk on the side of ships in zero gravity. He felt the pull, his upper body wanting to be drawn through the hatch, but his feet remained planted.

But he also couldn't move fast, no where near as fast as he wanted. If both feet left the ground, he would fly through that hatch just the same as Trace and the captain.

He reached the console and got to work, but something was wrong. He tried to close the inner hatch, but an error sound blared in his ears. *Come on.* He tried a different approach. Same sound, causing him to flinch. What the hell did they do to this thing? He wasn't a computer guy. What the hell did he know about fixing it?

But lives counted on him, on them, getting that hatch closed. He tried the outer hatch. The sound blared again, causing him to flinch once more. "Captain, what's your override password?" he demanded into the radio in his helmet.

"Mila," came the answer through the speaker.

Avery typed in the override password, mentally crossing his fingers, hoping it would work.

He got a new screen. *Different's good.* He resisted the urge to count the seconds. *How long does she have left?* He found a master override for the inner hatch and activated it.

The door closed, sealing with a hiss, and the constant pressure dragging him toward the entry ceased. He sighed. But it wasn't over yet.

"Do you have her, sir?"

"Almost."

Avery and Braddock waddled to the small viewing window in the hatch, knocking heads together before remembering they didn't need the helmets anymore. They took them off in unison, too concerned to even smirk at the comedy of the situation.

The captain had Trace in his arms now. She wasn't moving. How long had she been out there? Could it have been ninety seconds already? "I don't suppose you bothered to count the seconds," he said.

Braddock shook his head, matching worry decorating his face. They looked back, breath held as the captain held tight to their comrade and propelled as fast as the suit would take him toward the ship. *Come on. Come on.*

Right before the captain entered the hatch, Avery waddled back to the control panel, just in case the one in there didn't work. He wasn't taking any chances. *Come on.*

They stood in perfect stillness, waiting, praying.

Tristan waited as the outer door slowly closed. Too slow. He clutched the immobile Mila to his chest even tighter. *Don't die on me. You can't die on me.* The door closed and the second one opened.

He stumbled in and laid Mila on the ground at Braddock's feet. Tristan yanked the helmet off and ripped the top half of the suit off so fast he probably damaged it, not that he cared. He dived at Mila. He had to get her breathing again. Before it was too late.

He started CPR, knowing she would never make it to the med bay. They didn't have that much time. *Breathe, baby.* He counted silently, then checked her pulse. No heartbeat. *Don't do this.* He counted again, then went back to breathing for her. Time drew out to eternity as he alternated between breathing for her and pumping her heart for her.

Braddock had never liked Trace, but she didn't deserve to die like that. She'd proved her worth, repeatedly, above and beyond the call of duty. She was a pilot and yet she'd helped with the investigations, fought beside them.

A part of his mind whispered that she wouldn't be dead, dying, right now if she'd bothered to follow orders. But another part whispered they might all be dead if she had. Would they have closed the hatch if she hadn't run ahead? They would have gone against those men and they couldn't fight back in the suits.

He looked on with pity as the captain worked over her body. He felt stupid for not realizing how much the woman meant to his superior officer until he saw him crying over her just then.

As she took a breath, allowing them to breathe easily once more, his gaze was drawn to her hands, which curled under with that first breath. But he could have sworn they looked more like claws.

Had his mind been playing tricks on him?

CHAPTER THIRTY-SEVEN

"What happened?" Mila asked.

"You nearly died," Tristan said from beside her.

She opened her eyes and turned her head to him, too exhausted to even sit up. Sitting in a chair beside her bed, he looked as exhausted as she felt. "I gathered."

"Or maybe it's more appropriate to say you did die."

The pain in his eyes forced the next words out of her as if comforting him was as vital as breathing. "I'm sorry."

"Just don't do it again," he said with a weak smile that almost reached his eyes.

"Aye aye, captain." She tried to raise an arm in salute—sarcastically, of course—but both arms felt like they'd been nailed to the bedding.

He shook his head and reached for her hand, rubbing it soothingly. She closed her eyes and almost groaned.

"Is the danger over?"

"I don't know. I have security officers scouring the area surrounding the ship, but we haven't been able to find anything but dead bodies. We also have men guarding each of the airlocks. They won't get back on board," he said fiercely.

"Good," she said and fell back to sleep.

The next time she woke, she was alone. Her strength had returned somewhat and she could sit, even if it wore her out. She lifted herself upright, breathing heavily, letting the burn in her arms settle. She had a bandage on her right arm and another on her torso.

Jeez, I keep getting shot.

She could make out the whispering of voices outside her room, but no words.

As she breathed, her lungs felt worn, tired. Other than that and the bullet holes, she felt fine. "At least the headache's gone."

Without distractions, her mind kept flitting back to those terrible moments before she lost consciousness. Holding on for dear life. Her heart started to speed up. Losing her grip. She felt it pounding in her temples, making her breathe more rapidly. Breathing, but suffocating. Panic. She grabbed her chest as she struggled for breath. Her chest hurt.

An alarm sounded and people rushed into the room. They crowded around her as her world narrowed into a place where only escape mattered. Voices and movement surrounded her in a surreal amalgam of sensations, then everything became heavy, her heart slowing until she passed out.

When she woke again, Tristan was back.

"Heard you had a panic attack."

Amusement colored his voice, so she did the only appropriate thing. She flipped him the bird. He laughed and she looked over as he shook his head.

"Feeling better?"

"Yeah, strong as an ox." She flexed her arms like a muscle builder. "How long has it been?"

"A day or two."

She nodded, not letting it bother her how long she'd been out. "You find your bad guys yet?"

"We don't know if we found all of them, but we found their ships. Outside the gas-ring. The engineers think they can use the parts from the fighters to repair the engine. That is, if we can tow them back to the Orleans."

"That's good, I guess."

"You've got some friends who'd like to see you."

She smiled, a little excited. She'd forgotten her earlier fear. Not knowing who made it and who didn't.

Tristan got up and walked to the door, opening it for Luke, then Avery, Braddock, and Santos.

She laughed. "Half of them don't even like me."

"May!" Luke said, bouncing through the door and assaulting her with a hug.

She winced, his arm wrapping around her bandages like a vice. He didn't notice, but she breathed easier when he loosened up and leaned back to get a better look at her.

"You look good, considering," Luke said, winking at her playfully.

"Considering? I look damn good."

"Good to see you back in the world of the living," Avery said.

Braddock just looked at her suspiciously, like he expected her to do God only knew what. It unnerved her, causing a sinking feeling in her gut.

"What are *you* doing here, Santos?"

She shrugged. "Just checking to see how much longer I'll have the room to myself."

"But, of course."

"Of course."

They talked and caught up, reveling in their individual stories of daring deeds. Mila kept quiet. Everyone knew what she'd done. And if they didn't, she felt no need to tell them. She couldn't slip back into the shadows, but she had no intention of grabbing the spotlight either.

Eventually, Tristan started in on them about lazing about and not doing their jobs and the crowd dispersed. "You'll be all right on your own?"

"Yeah. Never better."

"No more panic attacks?"

"Probably not."

He paused, maybe because she hadn't given him the absolute assurance he wanted, but eventually leaned in, kissed her forehead, and said, "Until later."

208

No quantity of doctors, nurses, and miscellaneous medical personnel could keep Mila there indefinitely. Food and rest did her a world of good and soon she wanted, no needed, to flee the well-meaning medical staff. She slipped out of bed a few times. Even got as far as the door before someone would ask her what she was doing out of bed and guice her back to her "rightful" spot.

But she wasn't tired anymore. Other than two still healing holes in her, she was just fine. And she needed to move. Now.

Unfortunately, there were no real night shifts on a spaceship. No shift was lighter than the rest personnel-wise. So she couldn't just wait until a shift change or something. Or could she? Didn't shift changes tend to be somewhat chaotic? Maybe she could slip out when people were distracted.

She went back and sat on the bed, twiddling her thumbs and watching the clock tick the seconds by. *God, the med bay is so boring.* She needed to *do* something. Desperately.

She'd almost nodded off when she heard a commotion outside. People moving around, murmurs of voices. Shift change. She got up, and walked out boldly. *Better not to look suspicious.* Nobody noticed her. Of course, she'd already slipped on her somewhat ragged and bloodstained uniform. It was better than the alternative.

She turned and headed toward the exit, her heart in her throat the entire time. People bumped into her, mumbling "Excuse me" and "Sorry" as they went. *A few more feet.*

Freedom was in sight when someone called, "Hey, you're not supposed to be out of bed."

She ignored the voice, picking up her pace and pretending the person had been talking to someone else.

"Hey, wait!"

Mila shoved the doors open and made a mad dash down the hallway. She reveled in the feel of her muscles, in being able to stretch and work them, in the freedom of movement, the lack of claustrophobia.

Admittedly, she was still on a ship. It was still enclosed. But the long expanse of hallway felt enormous compared to being trapped in that bed, in that room, for days.

Her feet took her where they would and she found herself outside the engine room. She slipped in, noticing the lack of doors and the melted metal around the door frame. The engine room was still a whirlwind of activity as people tried to get the ship moving again.

This is even better than the hallway. She smiled and sat down, cherishing the vastness of the room. Everything would be all right. She just knew it.

"You're supposed to be in the med unit," Tristan said right next to her ear before sitting down beside her.

She shrugged. "And? You gonna throw me over your shoulder and drag me back there?"

"No. Feeling better, I guess?"

"I ran all the way here."

"Feeling that good, huh?"

"That good. People like me bounce back pretty quickly. And the injuries weren't really that bad."

"You were shot in the chest. Again."

"Getting to be a habit, isn't it?" She tried to joke, but the glare he gave her said he didn't appreciate it. "Sorry."

"It's all right. I'm probably not in the best of moods."

"What's wrong?"

"Besides you almost dying?"

She smiled. "Yeah, besides that."

He waved his hand in front of him. "We're still dead in the water. We don't know if all the enemy forces are dead. And I just got the final reports back from the attack."

"How bad?" She knew it had to be bad.

"We lost nearly a third of our crew."

Everything in her body seemed to sink, drain down. A third? She shook her head, trying to be professional, even though she'd never quite been in the military. She could have used that now. "Can we still man the ship?"

"I think so, but it'll be tight. You're the only surviving pilot, which will slow us down immensely."

She nodded, trying to work out in her head how many hours a day she could fly the ship safely. And trying to force out the images of the two pilots she'd only met in passing. The faces, smiles, sometimes haggard, kept flitting across her mind. "Are there any duty stations vacant?"

"A few, but that can't be helped. There's some overlap in proficiencies, but I'm still not sure we'll be fully covered in places."

She nodded again. "Maybe you should be going over personnel records. Planning out new duty rosters."

"Probably and I should be filling out KIA reports. I'm not looking forward to that."

"Do you want some help?"

The look on his face seemed hopeless. "Not now. You should get some sleep."

She rolled her eyes. "I've had enough sleep. I've been sleeping for days. What I need is something to do."

"You won't let me mope, will you?"

"Nope. Come on. We've got work to do." She dragged him to his feet and out of the engine room.

CHAPTER THIRTY-EIGHT

The following days passed too quickly, and far too slowly. There simply wasn't enough work to keep them from thinking of the crew they'd lost. It didn't help that Mila had assigned herself the task of filling out the KIA forms and uploading them into the TAT.

Mila worked across from Tristan as he planned the new duty rosters, moving people around to cover everything, which was impossible. She was the only person left on board with any piloting experience. She wondered how much longer until they reached their destination. How much farther was it?

She'd assigned herself twelve-hour shifts, much to Tristan's dismay.

"Nobody works twelve-hour shifts," he'd said.

But she wouldn't be moved. Twelve hours wasn't an unreasonable length for a shift, and it gave them an extra four hours of flight time they wouldn't have otherwise. She just hoped the engineers got the engine fully operational. If they only flew half the time *and* at a snail's pace, they would never get there.

But eventually, engineers reported to Tristan, stating the

engine was ready. They fired it up and the ship came off emergency power for the first time since she could remember. It was nice not seeing everything through dim, red light. They got comms back up and running next and she didn't even realize the temperature was back to normal. Not until Luke pointed it out, stretched in an ecstatic sprawl.

***

Mila had on a new, clean uniform. She'd viciously ripped off her bandages, declaring to no one in particular that she didn't need them anymore. She had a smile on her face, winked at Tristan as she passed his chair, and sauntered up to her place, ignoring the dirty look Braddock gave her.

Mila caressed the controls like a lover. *We meet again.* Sitting down felt like coming home. She'd been born to do this. She started the pre-flight checks. On some level, she registered the lack of people and it made her heart hurt. Only one communications officer instead of three, no one on radar. She could see the navigation officer straddling her seat to see both her console and the one beside her.

This trip has been hell.

When the checks were complete, she turned to Tristan. "Ready, captain."

"Then let's go."

She turned and took off, navigating out of the gas-ring and back into open sub-space.

***

Braddock stood at the back of the bridge, hands clasped firmly behind his back. He kept running the scene over and over again in his head. Had his eyes played tricks on him? His gaze landed suspiciously on their pilot, Trace. He admitted to himself that it didn't matter, at least at the moment, whether she was what he thought or not. Without a pilot, they would still be stuck.

He shifted his gaze away and to their captain, who stared moony-eyed at the probable shifter. He would get no aid from their captain, he was sure.

Days were long, arduous, but they reached their destination. Mila dropped the ship out of sub-space shortly before the alien world she knew so little of. Probably, she knew even less than the average person. She'd always tried to keep her nose down, and avoiding people and everything associated with them, including the news, had become second nature to her.

Her hands flew over the controls, docking the POS to the orbital space station above the planet covered in purple clouds. She felt a slight jerk as the ship locked in, giving her a stunning view of a purple planet.

"I heard it was caused by iodine gas in the upper atmosphere," Luke said.

Mila turned to him. "Really? It's stunning."

"Yeah, makes all the mess worth it, doesn't it?"

"Not really. We almost died repeatedly. I could make do without a purple sky."

He laughed, smiling at Mila, but the smile wasn't as big or bright as usual.

"So, want to go check out some aliens?"

"They probably don't appreciate people gawking at them."

"And?"

"I've got work to do," Mila said, returning to her responsibilities, even if it was an excuse. She would finish locking this POS up in a matter of minutes, but Luke didn't need to know that. "Go on ahead. I know you want to."

"All right. Later." He jumped up, slapped her on the back, and raced around the people leaving the bridge.

I'll never have that kind of energy.

After a few minutes, she'd set the stabilizers and powered down the engines. She turned around, but Tristan had already left. She hadn't realized she'd been smiling until her face fell. *He has stuff to do, silly.*

Tristan led the diplomats to the airlock, followed by a parade that included some of his own crew, most likely only coming to ogle some aliens. A small quiver ran through him as he opened the airlock, his mind flashing to Mila there, holding on for dear life, losing her grip, falling.

The doors slid open and he took a breath to calm himself, even if no one had noticed his distress. In the doorway stood a handful of aliens. Seeing them left his mind blank, his vocabulary failing him. They were alien in every sense of the word.

They made a writhing gesture he assumed was a greeting. The gesture seemed boneless, body and limbs rotating in a swirling pattern. It couldn't be matched by a human. He could only imagine an octopus being able to replicate the limb movements, but octopi don't have bodies like these things. He couldn't figure out how they stayed upright, but they did. His mind flitted to something he'd heard once, that their planet had much less gravitational pull than Earth.

He caught the diplomats bowing behind his back before they came forward, carefully speaking in choppy English. The aliens didn't understand much English, but they'd learned some and their speech organs allowed them to use a broader range of sounds than humans. Humans couldn't speak their tongue.

The aliens spoke up, speaking in a series of guttural tones and clicks. The diplomats replied in English, thanking them for a warm welcome before filing past him. He watched as the reduced gravity of the space station had its effect on them, lightening their steps, causing them to float just a little as they bounced along. The airlock slid shut behind them.

Now, to wait.

CHAPTER THIRTY-NINE

"Back to work, everyone," Tristan barked as he turned. "Nothing to see here."

Someone laughed, but they drifted off. He walked through the halls, making his way back to the bridge. When he got there, he stood in the doorway, watching Mila stare out the windows at the planet below.

"Beautiful, isn't it?"

She jumped. "Jesus, Tristan."

"Sorry." He crossed the bridge and sat in the seat beside her.

"It is beautiful, but so is Earth."

"Yeah." Right about now, he wanted nothing more than to be back on terra firma. Earth. This had been one hell of a tour. And it was only half over.

"So, how were the aliens?"

"Weird. Big. Black. Wriggly. Friendlier than humans." He shook his head at the last one, feeling ashamed of his species. *Homo sapiens sapiens*. He looked over at Mila, wondering if she considered herself human. Was she? And how much of the lore surrounding shifters was true. For all he knew, they were kinder, gentler, and more honorable than humans could ever be. "Tell me about shifters."

She looked over at him. "There's not much I can tell you. It's not like I've met a whole lot of them. I'm not that old for a shifter and I suspect the current political climate has scattered our already small community to the four corners of the Earth."

"I'm sorry."

"You didn't make policy, Tristan. You've been very under-standing."

"Thanks. Anyway, I imagine, even if you don't know as much as some, you certainly know more than I do."

"I guess so," she hedged. "What do you want to know?"

"Is it true that shifters tend to be assassins and thieves?"

"Maybe, I don't know, but I doubt it's from a lack of moral fiber. In that respect, we're just like any human. Some are good, others aren't. Personally, I think it's more culture and opportunity. Keep in mind, being a mercenary wasn't such a bad thing a few hundred years ago. And many people stole because they had no other way of living. Survival is a strong instinct.

"And well, after a while, if that was their options, I think the shifter communities would become ingrained, some in normal ways, but some in less socially acceptable ones."

"How is it you don't know your own people?"

"I didn't know I was a shifter, that I would become one. It just happened one day. Well, you know the story."

"Yeah." He paused, deep in thought. "So, what can you do? What can't you?"

She smiled. "Lots." She rubbed her hands together and glanced at the door. "You know, if we lock that door, I can show you."

"Okay." He got up, and his fingers roamed over the panel, closing and locking the door. "Good to go."

Mila's smile grew bigger as she stood and held one finger up. "Shifter rule number one: we can only shift into something of the same mass. Tigers are one of the best choices for an animal, as few others carry similar bulk to humans."

She stood back by the consoles and chairs, hesitant for a second. Nervous on more than one level, she pulled off most of her clothes and shifted effortlessly into a tiger, migrating excess iron to her paws so she didn't float. Slinking to Tristan in that limp-limbed stalk large cats are known for, she rubbed up against him, her head reaching his hip and let out a gentle roar.

Tristan laughed, his hand reaching down and petting her, rubbing the top of her head, behind her ears, between her shoulder blades.

Good God, that feels good.

She sat and leaned into his hand, sending him off balance. A coughing laugh slipped from her as Tristan regained his footing. With a great yawn, she stood, crossed the room to her clothes, and shifted back to the shape of May Trace.

She ticked off more "rules" on her fingers and dressed again. "Rule number two: we can't immediately identify one of our own. Rule number three: we need calories to power a change, so if we shift, we have to eat.

"Shifting between genders is weird. I don't like doing it. It is by far the most disturbing sensation possible.

"I never have to diet. Between higher caloric need and the ability to shift fat cells into muscle mass, it's not a concern. Which is wonderful, because I love to eat.

"We tend to prefer one or a couple forms. Contrary to popular belief, we don't constantly shift from one form to the next. I spend almost all of my time in the face I've had since birth."

"What *do* you look like? I can't believe I never wondered that before."

"Okay." And suddenly, Mila felt nervous, like she was stripping down armor right before battle, more nervous than when she'd stripped in front of him. *What if he doesn't like the real me?* She took a deep breath and shifted back into herself, closing her eyes, afraid to see his reaction.

"Beautiful," he breathed.

She smiled, eyes still closed. "Not disappointed?"

"Never."

"Avery."

He looked up from his desk. "Yeah, lieutenant?"

"Can I have a word?"

"Certainly. Come on in."

Braddock walked in, shutting the door behind him. He looked around the tiny, near empty office. "What do you think of May Trace?"

Curiosity in his eyes, Avery said, "I think she's brave, dedi-
cated, and the best damned pilot I've ever seen." He leaned
forward, elbows on his desk. "Why?"

"She's rubbed me wrong from day one. There's something not
right about her."

"Braddock, that something not right you're feeling is just
your stick-up-your-butt mentality when it comes to military
command. Ease up on the girl."

"That's not it." *Not completely.* "I think I've found her secret."

"Secret?" Nothing piqued Avery's interest like a secret.

"Yes, a secret."

"And what secret might that be?" Avery still sounded skeptical.
Not for long.

"I think she's a shifter."

CHAPTER FORTY

Avery burst out laughing, pounding away at the desk as tears formed at the corners of his eyes. Little fits of laughter continued taking him by surprise but he could breathe easier as he wiped the tears from his face. "You have one hell of an active imagination, lieutenant. I wouldn't have suspected. Not in a thousand years."

Braddock puffed up, outrage turning his face red.

Holy shit, he's dead serious.

"I do *not* have an active imagination. I know what I saw."

Avery froze. *Saw? What did he see?* He raised an eyebrow at Braddock, apprehension seeping into his brain. He didn't want to believe what the lieutenant was saying. Trace? A shifter?

"The day the airlock was breached. After the captain brought her back on board. I saw her hands. Only they weren't hands, they were claws."

Avery sat back, tapping his fingers against the top of his desk.

"You do realize the implications of your testimony, don't you?"

Braddock nodded. "I do."

"She's our pilot. Our *only* pilot." Not to mention he'd started seeing her as a friend. Sitting there, staring back at Braddock, he found himself in an unprecedented position.

He didn't want to uphold the law.

Mila was walking back to her bunk after a long round of poker. She yawned, her eyes closing and tearing as she bumped into someone. "Oh, sorry. Avery."

"I need to speak with you privately." He looked grim.

"Sure." She nodded and let Avery into her tiny room. "Have a seat."

But he didn't. He paced a couple times before taking up a position on the opposite wall and leaning against it, arms crossed. "Don't lie to me. Your livelihood might depend on your answer."

"Okay…" Now, she was worried. *What the hell's going on?* The old anxieties fired up again and she fought a sudden urge to dash for the door.

"Are you a shifter?"

Her mouth opened, but no words came out. *This is not happening! Ten years without a single person finding out. A few weeks on this POS and I feel like half the ship knows.* Collecting herself, she said, "How do you expect me to answer that?"

"With the truth." He glared, his stance getting harder, implacable.

"Avery, I like you. Respect you. You're a good guy. But I don't know how to answer that question." She waved her hand in the air. "This whole thing with shifters is just a great big witch hunt. And I can't help thinking someone has it in for me and aimed you my way. That's what happened, isn't it?"

Mila saw the truth in his eyes. And she could guess who, too.

"Lieutenant Braddock?" Although how Braddock had figured out her secret, she might never know.

"How did you know?"

She shrugged. "He's the only one on this boat who doesn't like me, besides that assassin earlier."

"Still, Trace," he shook his head, "Braddock isn't the type to lie… or see things."

What the hell did he see?!

He stood, waiting, arms across his chest. "I'm not leaving without an answer."

What do you do when your entire life hangs in the balance? When a single person's opinion can have devastating effects and you don't know what to do? She had a strong urge to cry. She felt that pressure of emotion building up, but she dared not let it loose.

The silence built between them and in the end it was the look of disappointment in his eyes that loosened her tongue. "Yes."

He let out a sigh and his entire posture relaxed. "This is bad."

"Yeah. What are you going to do?"

"I suspect Braddock would have me lock you up, sooner rather than later."

"And will you?" She couldn't breathe, needing the answer before life could go on.

"No. I don't know what the hell we're gonna do, but I won't lock you up. In my eyes, you're a damned hero, Trace." He paused. "Is Trace even your real name?" His face paled several shades as another realization hit him.

"No, my name isn't Trace and no, I didn't kill her. That bastard assassin did. But when I showed up here, he thought he hadn't finished the job." A humorless laugh slipped out. "So many people died because of my stupidity."

"What do you mean?"

She looked up at him. "If I hadn't taken over her identity, the assassin wouldn't have been here. He wouldn't have killed all those people."

Avery crossed his arms once more, his brow furrowed. "That's not your fault. Or maybe I should say, it's the lesser of two evils. Yeah, he came here because of you. But, because of you, we learned of the plot to sabotage this mission. Because of you, that assassin is now dead. He can't kill another living soul ever again."

"Really?"

"Really."

"Braddock's still a problem."

"He's a problem we can put off for another day."

"He could send word back to Earth, tell them what he thinks I am. They could be waiting for me when we land."

"We'll figure something out. I promise."

She nodded. "Tristan knows, too."

Avery smiled. "He does, does he? Why am I not surprised?"

Avery walked beside Trace, marveling at the fact he could walk beside a shifter and not think of all the propaganda that had been bandied about over the years. "What *is* your name?"

Trace looked around, checking for people. He imagined she had to develop a cautious streak. "Mila Anya Dragomirov."

"Russian?"

"Only by very distant heritage."

He nodded. It was like that a lot in America. Many families had been in the United States for centuries, but they still clung to their ancestry. They religiously chose ethnic names, ate the food, and spoke the language of the old country to the exclusion of all others. Every aspect of their lives laid testament to a culture and land their ancestors fled from desperately. It was… ironic.

"How did you end up with May Trace's identity?"

"She was my friend. She died," Mila breathed.

"How did she die? You said the assassin killed her."

"Well, not directly. He hired hoodlums to fake a mugging. I was there. They stabbed her, then took off. It was an arterial wound. She would have never reached the hospital. Even if I'd had the wits to call for help."

"I'm sorry."

"I just wish I hadn't wasted so much time. When I found out what I was, I ran. I didn't talk to her for ten years. We should have kept in touch. We should have…"

"Stop." He jogged out in front of her, stopping her with a palm to her chest. "Don't do that to yourself. Things happened the way they were meant to. You couldn't have changed things. You wouldn't have changed things. This is how they are. This is how they must be."

Her head sagged. "I know. But it doesn't stop me from wishing things had turned out differently."

"Would you have wished you'd never gotten to fly the Orleans? Never met the captain?"

"No!"

He smiled at her, letting his arm down. "See? How they're supposed to be."

She shook her head. "I like how you think."

He bowed. "At your service, madame."

They spent the rest of the walk in silence. He glanced over, seeing a small smile on her face. *Good.*

Tristan jerked his head up as the doors to his office slammed open, admitting Avery and Mila in a rather theatrical manner.

"We have a problem," Avery said. "Braddock suspects."

"Braddock suspects *what*?" He looked at Mila, but she gave nothing away.

Avery looked at Tristan, then at Mila. "Yeah, I know what she is. And if we don't come up with a game plan, so will everyone else."

Mila blanched, causing Tristan's heart to clench in his chest.

"Sit." He leaned back in his chair, using his role as captain to stay calm, be what he needed to be. "Tell me everything."

"Braddock came to my office today. Told me Trace was a shifter. I didn't believe him. Actually, I laughed in his face. Asked him if he realized the implications of the accusations he was making.

"He told me that when she came back through the airlock, her hands were in the form of claws. He didn't doubt what he claimed to see. And I was inclined to believe him. Braddock has no imagination.

"The way I see it, we have two options. Option one is prove she isn't a shifter." He looked over and winked at Mila. "Option two is make her disappear. Probably, list her among the dead. There would be no body and Braddock wouldn't be able to prove she hadn't died. Hopefully."

Tristan sat, thinking. He wanted to swear up and down the hallways, but that wasn't behavior befitting a captain. It would figure Braddock would be the threat to her. *Damned tight-assed gremlin.* He should have done more than give him a firm chastisement. "I doubt either option would work, Avery. Option two wouldn't work because people remember seeing her after the big fiasco. She's our only remaining pilot. That would require too much coverup. And how the hell would we manage option one?"

"Fake DNA testing."

He raised an eyebrow at his head of security. "Fake it *how*?"

"Swap samples. All I need is a female sample, bring it in to medical for testing. Say someone accused her of being a shifter. After everything that's happened, I'm surprised nobody has done it. There's certainly enough craziness to make people paranoid."

"And you think that would work?"

"Sure. If the head of security brings in a sample, they should assume I wanted to ensure the samples weren't swapped out. You know, like trying to pass drug testing by using someone else's urine. And we have buccal swabs in the security offices for collecting DNA evidence from suspects."

Tristan nodded. That could work. It had to. "Do it."

Avery stood. "Right away," and left.

"How are you holding up?"

She let out a shaky breath. "Like my whole world is falling apart."

"I imagine. Come here." He opened his arms, enticing her.

She gave him a small smile, walked over, and sat in his lap, snuggling into his chest. "Thanks," she whispered. "I needed that."

CHAPTER FORTY-ONE

*A*very felt he might jump out of his skin at any moment. He'd ordered "randomized" shifter screening, saying that after the fiasco with the assassin, it was warranted. Nobody argued as he collected buccal swab samples from a half-dozen people.

Behind closed doors, he took one of the female samples he'd collected and put it in a fresh envelop, this time changing the information. He filled out Trace's bio. Name, rank, ID numbers. Would someone be able to tell? Did they keep previous DNA tests on file? Damn, he wished he'd paid more attention to that side of the business.

He organized the stiff envelopes, wrapping a rubber band around them to keep them together. The bundle was a tight wad in his fist as he left his office. He scanned his surroundings, but nobody noticed. Everyone was on high alert after the events of this trip. There were probably still saboteurs on board, which really irked him. He felt confident they hadn't caught all of them. He wanted to catch them. Needed to.

He left the offices, his eyes scanning each and every face.

Paranoid, Avery. You're getting paranoid.

He knew it, but it didn't stop him from suspecting all those around him. He shook his head. All but Trace. He was putting his very career on the line for that woman. But he knew right from wrong. And turning her over to the authorities would be wrong. Trace, no, Dragomirov was a hero. And even if her real name would never get the recognition, he wanted to see that she didn't get punished instead.

He entered the med bay and walked up to the counter. "I've got testing to be done."

"Don't you have better things to do than give us more work?" The woman glared.

Yes, clearly this will be a walk in the park, he thought sarcastically.

He smiled, hoping to work his charms on the girl. She was pretty enough. It wouldn't be any hardship. He put his hand over his heart. "I didn't intend to make your job any harder than it already is. It's my job to protect and sometimes that means taking preventative measures."

"Like?" she asked skeptically.

"Like testing people for shifter DNA. With everything that's happened, I'm not taking any chances. Especially after that shifter ran rampant on the ship the last few weeks."

"There was a shifter on board?" she whispered, leaning forward.

"Oh yes. Nasty bastard. An assassin. Perpetrated a string of murders. He was killed, but I've got to cover my bases. You understand."

"I think I remember those. One of the officers had to bring in quite a few bodies, if I don't recall. Wasn't one found in the food freezer?"

"Yeah. He probably died before we ever took off."

"Lord have mercy."

He nodded. "Indeed. Now, any chance you could run these for me? Most of them are just checking security staff, random checks. The last one here," he flipped through the envelopes until he found the one with Trace's name on it, "is a case. Someone accused her of being a shifter That one's got priority."

She took the bundle and glanced at the last envelope, then looked up at him, shocked. "Trace? May Trace? Who the hell would accuse her of being a shifter?"

He smiled at the mama bear protectiveness he saw in the woman across from him. *Good, an ally.* "Yeah, that was my reaction too. I don't believe it for a minute, but Lieutenant Braddock wouldn't be placated. I had to follow up on it."

"Lieutenant Braddock?"

"Yeah, but to tell you the truth, I think it's all bullshit. Braddock's had it in for her since day one. I wouldn't be surprised if spite drove his accusations and nothing more."

She nodded. "Well, that makes more sense. Honestly, Trace a shifter? She's far too sweet. It's such a pity she ended up in here so often this trip."

"Well, that's what happens when you jump in the middle of things."

"Jump in the middle of things?"

"Yeah, I mean she didn't start out doing that. When it all started, she sort of got thrust into it. A friend of hers gave her information, without her knowledge I might add, which got an assassin on her butt."

"The shifter," she said, awed.

"Exactly. But since then, she's repeatedly shown no hesitance in entering the fray, even though it wasn't her job. She helped with investigations and helped fight off the invaders who nearly killed everyone on board by opening the airlock."

"Sounds like a hero to me."

"My thoughts exactly."

"Well, Avery."

"Kyle," he said.

Her smile grew. "Kyle. I will make sure these get done. ASAP. I don't want this hanging over our friend's head any longer than necessary." She patted his hand.

"You're an angel."

"Not hardly," she said with a wink.

Avery relaxed back into his office chair. At least that was taken care of. A knock sounded at his door. "But, of course," he muttered. He took a moment. "Come in."

Braddock stormed in.

"Ah, the prodigal son returns."

"Knock it off, Avery. I outrank you."

Avery glared, his frame going rigid. "What burr got in your claw, Braddock?"

"What have you done about Trace, *Avery*? I could have you brought up on charges for not doing your job, you know."

He gave it a beat before speaking, surprised by the anger in the superior officer's voice. "You need to stop with the threats, Braddock. I *am* doing my job. Even overworked as we are, I'm still checking your rather ridiculous accusations of someone who will probably be our most decorated crew member once we arrive on Earth."

"She doesn't deserve any fucking metals. She's a damned shifter."

"Braddock, shut up," he shouted, getting to his feet. "Shifter or no, she has repeatedly saved the lives of this crew. She has gone above and beyond the call of duty. And you know what? If it turns out she *is* a shifter, however unlikely I find it, I think she would deserve it more."

Braddock stood, mouth agape.

"Because this wasn't her duty at all. She took it upon herself. No vows. No oaths. No contracts. I'll do my duty, *Braddock*. I've sent her DNA to med bay for testing. If she's a shifter, they'll figure it out. Now I'd appreciate it if you leave me and my men to more important matters, like finding the rest of those conspirators."

CHAPTER FORTY-TWO

Mila spent a lot of time on the bridge waiting. Being near her console, looking out over that odd purple planet, soothed her. *I wish I was flying. That would really soothe me.* But this first diplomatic talk wouldn't end for a few more days. It would be the first of many, Tristan had told her, but the first was often the most important.

She wasn't privy to what was going on and she didn't care. The purpose of this mission barely registered on her list of concerns right now. Instead, her mind kept flitting back to the testing she could almost feel being done. Would it work? Would they really believe the sample was hers?

"Everything will be all right," Tristan said, coming up behind her.

She jumped and turned, a smile slowly stretching her face. "Hey, Tristan." She sounded tired, even to her own ears.

"It'll be all right, don't you worry."

"I can't help but worry. Yet again, my life's on the line here. I'm getting tired of feeling that way."

"Miss your old life?"

"Yes and no. It was simpler. Safer. But it wasn't really living."

"It wasn't?"

"No, I just hid in a hole, passing my days with nothing. Certainly nothing of value, of importance. I'm doing something worthy now, even if it got me shot up in the process." She smirked at him, waving her hand in the general vicinity of her various wounds.

He walked to her, pulling her into his arms and reveling in how she squirmed closer. "You *are* important, Mila. And everyone will see that." He kissed her temple, then rubbed his cheek against her smooth skin.

"So long as Braddock's accusations don't encourage the people back home to test me again."

"They won't."

"They could. If Braddock insists again, they could."

"I won't let it happen, Mila."

She turned around in his arms, looking him straight in the eyes. "No matter how highly you think of yourself, you're not the master of the universe. There are people you have to report to, people *I* have to report to. If they ask me to get tested, my only option might be to run. And that might not be an option anymore."

"I'm not going to lose you, Mila."

Avery walked into Tristan's office, knocking this time. He chose to ignore Trace sitting in the captain's lap. "I've got the tests back. And the digits of a rather nice medical officer who just happened to appreciate my charms. Thanks for that, by the way. No red flags raised. Nobody questioned it. You should be safe."

"Thanks, Avery. What about Braddock?"

Avery crossed his arms. "Haven't talked to him yet. Not looking forward to that particular conversation. The last one didn't exactly go… smoothly. I didn't think he knew curse words."

"Well, I'm sure you can pull it off, what with all your *charms.*"

Avery shook his head and left, taking care to close the doors behind him.

"Avery," a belligerent voice snapped from down the hall.

Great.

"Yes, Braddock." He turned to the voice, again crossing his arms over his chest.

"What's the status on the Trace investigation?"

"Done. She's clear."

"What?" Braddock grabbed Avery by his shirt, lifting him off the ground. "What do you mean she's clear?"

Avery glared at the man holding him as his shirt dug into his armpits. He placed his feet against the wall and shoved, throwing Braddock off balance and onto the floor. With a single move, he flipped him, sending his knee into the other man's back. He leaned in to speak. "Never forget I'm Head of *Security.* I could wipe the floor with you, *lieutenant.* What deference I give you is due to rank alone and nothing more. Understand?"

"Yes," his opponent breathed.

"Good." He let up, standing and returning to his original position.

Braddock was slower to stand, but he glared from across the hall. Now, he stayed out of grasping distance. "I'll repeat my question. What do you mean she's clear?"

"I mean her test came back negative for shifter DNA. She's no different from you or me." And he couldn't believe he said that with a straight face.

"That's not possible."

"But unerringly true."

"It must be a false negative."

"It's not that kind of testing. There're no false positives and false negatives with DNA testing."

"It can't be! I saw!"

"Then maybe you should get yourself checked in somewhere when we get back, lieutenant." And it took great effort to hide his smile as he said it. He *really* didn't like this guy.

Braddock glared. "This isn't over."

Avery rolled his eyes. Of course it wasn't over. Why would it be over?

CHAPTER FORTY-THREE

*D*ays passed and they started their journey back home. It was slow, but quiet. Nothing serious happened, just Avery and his people rounding up the conspirators. At the times Mila saw him, he usually wore a scowl. He tried to smile for her, but she saw it irked him that he couldn't find the last of those behind the attacks on their ship.

She doubted they would ever find them all.

Days were long, exhausting, and she went straight to bed most of the time. Tristan still tried, and failed, to keep his distance, which was all right with her. She didn't know what to do with him either. She didn't have a lot of experience with relationships.

But nothing topped when that big blueberry they called Earth entered their horizon. She laughed and shouted when she saw it. The entire bridge stopped to watch. She could feel the collective sigh. It had been a long trip. Hard. A lot of people would be glad to be home. Even with possible exposure still flitting in the periphery of her consciousness, it felt good to see Earth again.

"Ready to enter atmosphere, captain," she said.

"At your leave, pilot."

She descended, feeling the massive POS pull toward the Earth. She charted their trajectory, planning a gradual decline that would have them looping the planet twice before setting down in Florida. They entered atmosphere and soon her vision turned red from the heat of reentry.

The controls pulled at her hands like a horse wanting its head. She held firm, feeling the subtle shake as the various forces warred against one another. Clouds passed and soon she made out things in the distance. A land mass. An ocean.

She adjusted the controls, slowing them further. They were almost there.

"Luke, communications."

"Roger."

He reached over and grabbed the short range radio two seats away. "Tower, this is U.S.S. Orleans. We are inbound west. Requesting permission for landing."

"Orleans, this is Tower. Cleared for straight in on One West."

"Roger." He put the radio down. "One West, sweet cheeks."

"I'd kick your ass right now for that name, but I'm busy."

He laughed. "I know. That's why I did it."

Mila didn't even have the opportunity to glare at him. She needed to focus straight ahead. She could see the landing strip now and adjusted her controls more.

Flaps, landing gear.

She felt the pull of the landing gear as they created more resistance.

Reduce speed.

They continued their descent.

Slower.

Closer.

Almost.

Touchdown.

The ship bumped. Once, twice, then coasted down the wide runway as she applied the brakes, slowing them to a stop.

She sighed, a smile on her face.

"Excellent landing, May," Luke said.

She punched him in the arm.

"Ow," he said, rubbing the spot.

"That's for the sweet cheeks comment."

"Beast," he grumbled.

"Come on. I think it's long past time we got off this POS."

"Damn straight."

<hr>

Luke bounced her way off the ship, skirting people like a fish through the sea. A grin stretched her face as she hopped off the ship, the enclosed space opening into the great outdoors. She looked around her, laughing at herself. As far as the eye could see, concrete, blacktop, and blocky buildings made up the landscape.

Well, maybe not the great outdoors…

Still, it was freeing to no longer be cooped up, no longer have a ceiling over her head or walls closing her in. She stepped away from the ship, searching for familiar faces. Her family had always been supportive, first with her differences and then with her career. That's how she'd gotten her nickname, after all. She'd told her family one time, "I'm lucky to have such a supportive family," and it stuck.

"Mom!" she squealing, taking off at top speed across the pavement. Behind her mom, her dad and siblings waited, big grins on their faces. Luke slammed into them, trying to hug them all at once and failing. "I've missed you guys."

"Welcome home," her dad said, echoed by her mom.

As she pulled away, her older brother took one look at her, clutched at his heart and said, "Gasp! You look like a guy!"

Luke threw her bag at him.

"Oomph," he said as he toppled to the ground. "What've you got in here? Bricks?"

"Wouldn't you like to know?" she said, sticking out her tongue at him.

God, it's good to be home.

The ship was a sea of commotion, everyone racing to gather their things and run into the arms of their loved ones. Mila took her time, taking the jostling she got from the people around her. *God, what if the whole crew had survived?!*

She reached her bunk with only a few bruises. Santos was already packed, her bag slung over one shoulder. "Hope I never see you again," Santos said.

"Likewise," she said with a smile.

Santos shook her head, but smiled too as she pushed past Mila and walked out.

Mila started shoving things in her bag, enjoying the weight of the objects once again. Gravity. Beautiful.

She zipped the bag, put it over her shoulder, and opened the door, only to be greeted by three men standing guard. "Can I help you?"

"May Trace?"

"Yeah?"

"You've been accused of being a shifter. Come with us."

CHAPTER FORTY-FOUR

Mila followed the men in abject terror. She could barely breathe. Suddenly, the same gravity she'd reveled in only minutes ago seemed amplified by the weight of the accusations against her, weighing her down, oppressing her.

She looked around her, searching, but couldn't find Tristan or Avery. Where were they? She could really use an ally right about now.

They led her into a small room with a table and two chairs, each chair on opposite sides of the table. Interrogation room. She tried to swallow the lump that had formed in her throat, but failed. It seemed determined to choke her.

She didn't sit. She was too nervous to sit. So she paced.

Time ticked by, only there was no clock. The room, the environment, seemed designed to simulate a complete stoppage of time. Was this what hell would be like? An eternity in a moment?

She continued pacing. It would be all right. They had records on the ship, DNA testing. Faked DNA testing. She would have testimony from Tristan, Avery. It would be all right.

The door opened and a man walked through. "Why so nervous, May Trace?"

She stopped her pacing. "Forgive me if I don't appreciate being trapped in a tiny room after being stuck on a ship for weeks. I'd rather hoped I'd be racing off toward my leave right about now, not pacing an interrogation room."

The man nodded and motioned her to sit as he did so himself. She did, watching him intently.

"Someone accused you of being a shifter, Pilot Trace."

"I know. We already had this investigation. On the ship."

"You did?"

"Yes. The Head of Security took buccal swabs. Had them tested. It came back normal. Lieutenant Braddock just has it in for me."

"Lieutenant Braddock?"

"That's who brought forward the accusations, isn't it?"

The man remained quiet. "I'll be back." He stood and left.

Avery waited outside the ship, watching people disembark, looking for someone in particular. He'd sent a text message to a friend, asking for a phone call. He spotted his quarry, "Faulk!"

The captain turned to him and changed course, though his head kept on a swivel.

"You won't find her," he said as the other man stepped up to him.

"What?"

"She was escorted off the ship by three MPs shortly after we landed."

"What?!"

Avery put up his hands. "It wasn't me. I can only assume it was your lieutenant. I don't have all the details yet." As if on cue, his phone rang. "I've got to take this." He pressed the icon to answer the call, "Speak."

"It's good to hear your voice, old friend."

"Likewise." He smiled. "We need to get together sometime. It's been too long."

"And yet, somehow I doubt that's why you called."

"It's not. Do you know anything about an investigation into a woman named May Trace?"

"Hold on." Clicking came over the line as his friend looked something up on his computer. "Accused of being a shifter?"

"That would be it."

"And you want the investigation terminated."

"The investigation was already terminated. We tested her on the Orleans and cleared her. She saved everyone on board the ship."

"I'll see what I can do."

"Thank you."

"You'll owe me for this."

Avery laughed. "Add it to my tab."

Mila's stomach growled. It felt hollowed out after a long shift, and an interminable length in the interrogation room. "For no fucking reason!" she yelled at no one, slamming a fist at the wall.

She couldn't sit still, alternating between sitting, lounging, standing, pacing, then sitting again every few minutes. Dropping her face onto her palm, she said to the empty room, "At this point, I'm too bored to be afraid. Couldn't they just bring me some fucking food? I'm half tempted to chew on the table at this point."

When did I last eat?

She looked to the door, almost daring it to open.

Tristan stayed glued to Avery's side. He wanted to tell him to fix it, but from the moment they landed, he was no longer Avery's captain and Avery was no longer his Head of Security.

"Name's Kyle. What about you?"

"Tristan." Did Kyle already know that? He couldn't remember. "How long will it take?"

Kyle shook his head. "As long as it has to. When you're calling in favors, it's best not to be picky."

Tristan nodded, but the non-answer didn't help his composure. He wanted to march over there and demand they release her. At this point, he wasn't even sure he would have cited the right reasons.

"Have some faith. We've done all we can. The military doesn't always move quickly and they aren't always just, but we've got logic on our side."

"If you say so."

If only he could make himself believe.

———

After what felt like three or four days, the man returned. "You can go."

"Thank God!" Mila said, jumping out of her seat. She raced out and Tristan stood there waiting for her. "Tristan!" She raced into his arms.

"Oomph. Careful, woman."

"Oh, shut up. You know you love it."

"That I do."

"Everything squared away, then?"

"Yeah. MPs got the testing we did aboard the Orleans. Trusted it was valid. Lieutenant Braddock is probably not going to be fit for active duty for quite some time, though."

"Why's that?"

"He keeps insisting he saw your hands, that they were claws. Since you're not a shifter, that's impossible. The mucky mucks will probably request a psych eval."

Mila frowned, relieved to be free, but she felt bad about Braddock. She didn't like him, but wasn't sure he deserved that.

"Come on," he said, grabbing her hand. "Let's get out of here."

She nodded, and let him lead her out of the blocky, institutional building. Once outside, they walked sidewalks lined with bright green grass as short as a Marine's haircut.

"After you, my lady," Tristan said with a flourish as they arrived at a big black truck at the curb.

Mila chuckled and grabbed the door, turning back to look at him. "It suits you."

"Why thank you, my lady," he said with a grin as he rounded the hood and sat in the driver's seat.

Mila buckled in, running her hand over the material, focusing on the texture against her fingertips as Tristan pressed a button to start the car. She looked out the window, at the dash, at her fingers, anywhere but at Tristan as her future opened before her.

Ten years on the run. She'd never thought about her future, only about surviving. She'd had no friends, no prospects, sometimes even no food. *I can't go back to that.*

"You're awfully quiet over there." Tristan pushed up the steering wheel and turned to her. "What's on your mind?"

She shook her head. "I don't know what to do."

"Mila? Look at me."

She turned to him, biting her lip.

"Stay with me."

"What?"

He smiled. "I said, 'Stay with me.' "

"I heard you. I can't stay with you."

He leaned closer. "Why not?"

She sputtered, her mouth flapping like a fish. "I just can't."

He shrugged, as if it meant nothing to him, but his eyes spoke differently. "Well, you can't return to the barracks. May's roommate is bound to notice a difference."

Mila blanched. She hadn't even thought of where she would live, about May having a roommate.

"That's why you should move in with me. Total privacy."

She glared. "Somehow I doubt it."

"I swear. Scout's honor." He threw up a two-fingered salute.

"Were you really a scout?"

"No, but it still counts, right?"

Mila scoffed, shaking her head. "Not really."

Then he got serious. "I won't push you into something you're not ready for, Mila. My place has two bedrooms."

"Okay."

<hr>

"I can't do this," Mila said from the passenger seat, idly fingering the medal in her lap, feeling like a fraud. Cringing, she remembered the awards ceremony where they praised "May Trace" for her valor and for going above and beyond the call of duty. She wanted to bury it in a drawer and forget it even existed. She wanted to run to the house and hide.

"You can't avoid this, Mila."

She glared at him. "Bite me." Pointing a finger at him, she said, "And you better stop calling me Mila. Other people might not notice or care, but May's parents aren't among them."

"Sorry." His smile came too damn fast for her to believe his sincerity. He opened the driver's side door and rounded the car, dragging her out. "You're just going to have to suck it up."

She glared at the back of his head, but he just dragged her ever onward. In no time, they stood at the door of May's childhood home and a cold sweat broke out on her forehead. "I don't want to do this."

Guilt ate at her. She shouldn't have done this. She shouldn't have taken May's identity. Why couldn't she have protected May? Saved her? Why hadn't May just *told* her what was going on? Why couldn't the ground just suck her up?

Bang, bang, bang.

She glared again at Tristan. *Traitor.*

Footsteps sounded beyond the door and a moment later, it burst open. "May! Get over here." May's mother wrapped her in a big hug and Mila smiled.

Okay, just a little while longer…

EPILOGUE

Shortly after landing…

He stepped off the ship, taking in his first breath of un-recirculated air in months. It felt good, even if the jostling as he exited the ship and his frustrations over the series of events made him want to strangle someone.

Again.

He hefted his pack a little higher on his shoulder and crossed the space with strong, efficient strides. The crowd dispersed in another direction and soon he turned a corner. Even with the ship's massive size, he could no longer see it. He scowled and kept going, walking up to a black sedan.

As he climbed into the backseat, dropping his bag on the seat beside him, the driver turned to him. "How'd it go?"

"It didn't." He looked out the window as they turned a corner, the people exiting the ship coming back into view. Leaning closer to the glass, he smirked. *Was that….* "May Trace," he mouthed as three MPs frog marched her from the ship, a just outcome for someone who seemed to take a personal interest in derailing his plans.

"Don't you worry, boss. That was only half the negotiations, right?"

"Right. This was just a minor setback."

May Trace wouldn't be there next time.

He would be ready.

***

Thank you for reading Mila's Shift. I hope you enjoyed it.

Please consider leaving a review or rating the book.

And if you would like to read more from me, consider joining my mailing list at www.theeternalscribe.com.

You'll get:

An Exclusive copy of Mila's Flight (See Below)

Plus…
Giveaways | Discounts & Sales
Book Release Dates & Pre-Orders | Sneak Peeks
Advance Reader Copies | Bonus Content

***

MILA'S FLIGHT

Mila has dreamed of becoming a space pilot all her life. Today, she takes her sub-space qualifications, the last step toward her dream.

Then, as her friend drags her from bar to bar to "celebrate," something goes heinously wrong. It's cold, she's falling over drunk, and these men won't take no for an answer. At least, not until she changes and scares them away. She's terrified and alone, lost in a body she doesn't understand, unable to find herself again. But even when she shifts back, she's still trapped, lost. Shape shifters have no future, especially not in the military.

So she runs.

Only, the streets hold their own dangers. Someone is following her, and even a sound beating doesn't deter him. What does he want? And how does he keep finding her?

As paranoia and trust issues mix with the grief of lost dreams and separated loved ones, Mila must find her way, find herself, before it's too late.

SUPPLEMENTARY INFORMATION

Computer Systems

While more modern hard drives and monitors do not feel significant impacts from magnetic fields, the age of the ship developed for this book and the variability in the magnetic field generated for the MAG GRAV system can result in EMP-like effects, although on a much smaller scale. Over prolonged periods of time, this can cause damage to systems from additive effects. For this reason, the NSS moved to a centralized computer system with remote access points.

MAG GRAV

Zero gravity-related bone deterioration is caused by the body not having sufficient force applied to it. The system uses electromagnetic floor plates. Ferromagnetic thread is woven in cloth throughout the ship and ferromagnetic metals are used in the manufacture of all harder surfaces. The specific strength of the magnetic force is important, as it is directly correlated to the level of bone deterioration and as such, it is important that the properties of the garments utilized are comparable regardless of size of the wearer.

QuiKit

This is a technology that currently exists (though I came up with the name). It is used in 3rd world countries to provide inexpensive testing to locals. These kits are usually antibodies bound to a paper-like substrate that will change color based on presence of molecules that will bind to the antibodies.

Shape-shifting (Physiology)

Amoeba and other amorphous organisms are capable of changing shape to escape threats and reach food sources. While it would be theoretically possible for shape-shifters to exist (though none do in higher organisms), they would need to have evolved along a separate evolutionary path.

Shape-shifters have loosely structured tissues with easy to replicate designs. Further, not all tissue types are capable of shape-shifting. Some examples include: brain and spinal column, heart, primary arteries and veins, and most of the tissue in the digestive system and lungs. These systems serve as control points to power and feed the systems and tissues as they change.

Much of the shape-shifting capability arises at the tissue level. Shape-shifters have a simplified musculoskeletal system. The hard structure of bones in shape-shifters is caused by structures in the cells themselves rather than the tissues. The cells are connected together with chemical compounds easily dissolved with an enzymatic reaction triggered by shifting. The chemical reforms once the enzymatic activity ceases. The same holds true for muscles, tendons and ligaments.

Unlike many cells in higher organisms, shape-shifter cells have cilia designed to move them against each other mid-shift. This allows cells to reform into different-shaped tissues (e.g. shorter and wider bones, longer muscle groups).

Shape-shifting (Reproduction)

An important element in this series is the idea that shape-shifters can be born from human parents and go unknown. Shape-shifters are a separate species and are not inherently human or mutants. Female shape-shifters have unique characteristics in that they are capable of reproducing with *any* species. This is handled by specialized pathways active in oocytes and early stage fetuses. Female shape-shifters produce specialized recombinases during oocyte genesis (meiosis). When the cell is fertilized, it recognizes shifter-related genes, matching them with genes in the male chromosomes (if available). If unavailable, polymerases work with the recombinase to duplicate the shifter genes into the male chromosomes, which is effective since shifter genomes do not have sex-specific epigenetic markings. During the first few weeks of growth, the fetus will use target-specific silencing methods to turn off male-contributed genes that do not work in single copy and would otherwise cause termination of the fetus.

Sub-space travel

The sub-space travel system documented in this book is an adaptation of the Einstein-Rosen Bridge. There are a great many theories as to how an Einstein-Rosen Bridge might work. Some theories postulate that it connects two points in space-time (i.e. two points in the same universe). Others postulate that it could form a bridge between neighboring universes. This concept, regardless of how it is hypothesized, is very interesting as it is the only feasible means of interstellar travel currently postulated.

I took a great deal of liberty in coming up with this method of travel, though there are other more likely scenarios such as a bridge connecting two points in space, or even a significant time difference on each side of the bridge.

The most important part of this technology is the capability of forming these bridges, which I didn't provide any details into. At present, humanity has not discovered any of these bridges, and as such, we would not be able to learn enough about them to create one. I imagine, though, once we're discovered one and studied one, learning to create and control them will be right around the corner.

TAT system

This system is a logical extension of the Tachyonic Antitelephone thought experiment postulated by Albert Einstein in 1907. Tachyons are theoretical particles that can only move faster than the speed of light. In fact, the slower they get, the more energy is required (the inverse of normal matter). For this reason, particles that work similarly would be ideal for communication between interstellar distances. Because of the risk of breaking causality, the energy applied to the tachyons is very important in relation to the distance traveled. However, if those calculations are applied adequately, it would be theoretically possible to generate instantaneous communication across any distance. Please note: Tachyons are theoretical and have largely been deemed physically impossible (i.e. have had no scientific verification), however the beauty of science is the unknown, and we will likely never know all there is to know about the universe.

ABOUT THE AUTHOR

Danielle Forrest is a Paranormal SciFi author and Medical Laboratory Scientist based out of Indianapolis, IN.

Sign up for her mailing list at www.theeternalscribe.com to get access to exclusive content and updates.

facebook.com/theeternalscribe

twitter.com/theternalscribe

goodreads.com/theeternalscribe

instagram.com/theeternalscribe

amazon.com/author/danielleforrest